The Deadly Art of Deception

A Caribou King Mystery

by

Linda Crowder

Copyright 2016 by Linda Crowder

For information, email **Cozy Cat Press**, cozycatpress@aol.com or visit our website at: www.cozycatpress.com

COZY CAT
P R E S S

ISBN: 978-1-939816-97-9

Printed in the United States of America

Cover design by Paula Ellenberger
www.paulaellenberger.com

1 2 3 4 5 6 7 8 9 10

Dedication:

To my amazing family. Without your constant encouragement, I would never have been able to come this far.

Thanks!

Linda

Chapter 1

Icy-blue sea, rugged mountains, eagle drifting in an endless Alaskan sky, brown bear just emerging, lumbering toward the shore, body hidden by a boulder deposited some long ago day by a retreating glacier. Studying the play of light and shadow, I could almost feel myself standing on the shoreline, as much a part of the landscape as the rocks and the trees.

"It's a little plain, don't you think?" The woman's nasal tone snapped me back to reality. I was standing a respectful step behind my customers, ready to answer questions but never pressing. I'd shown them four paintings, but one was too big, another too small. A collage of native totems was pronounced too colorful, and this nature scene was too plain. A wild thought danced through my mind about how I'd like to respond to her, but I maintained a practiced, neutral appearance. I'd been running The Broken Antler Gallery for three seasons, and I knew buyers sometimes disparaged a work as a ploy to negotiate a lower price.

"I like it," said her husband. I felt a rush of fondness for him but kept my expression reserved. Had he come in alone, he would have bought the first painting he saw and tomorrow morning I'd be crating it up for shipment to their home in Hoboken, New Jersey. Instead, we'd spent the past twenty minutes trudging from painting to painting, looking for the elusive one that might satisfy his wife. I'd begun to despair that they would buy anything at all. I let my eyes wander to the other couples who were milling around the exhibit space, debating whether it was time to extricate myself from New Jersey and seek a more promising state.

"It's more than we wanted to spend," said the wife, drawing my attention back to her. She was more formally dressed than most of the visitors we had in Coho Bay. While her husband was wearing jeans and a brown leather bomber jacket, she was dressed in delicate fawn-colored slacks with a vibrant green and gold silk blouse and matching jacket. She was perhaps a bit older and a tad rounder than the designer had in mind for the outfit, but she wore it well, and I felt a twinge of envy.

The shift in tone caught me by surprise. Apparently her husband's opinion carried more sway than I'd supposed. I was happy they were going to buy, but I kicked myself for misjudging them. When you make your living selling big-ticket items, it pays to recognize the signals that separate buyers from bystanders. I had artists who were counting on me for their livelihood, and I took that responsibility seriously.

"I'm sorry to hear that," I said, my pulse picking up a beat. "What were you hoping to spend?" The price of art is negotiable, and I made it comfortable for buyers to make an offer if they liked an artist's work but not the price tag. Between what the artists hoped to get and what I knew they would accept for a work was a sweet spot where all parties would feel they got a fair deal.

"I was thinking five hundred."

I hid my irritation. I know that some people feel the need to start with a low-ball offer because it's the only way they feel they've gotten the best price. If they started higher and I accepted, they'd feel like they left money on the table. Still, there's low and then there's insultingly low, and her bid was insulting. "This is an original work by a well-known and respected artist. I couldn't accept less than three thousand."

"What about the first one?" asked the husband before his wife could make a counter-offer.

"The one with the view of Denali? I could accept eight hundred for that one. It's the first year I've exhibited that artist, so she's just starting to make a name for herself. Her work has been so well received I doubt you'll find such a low price by next year."

"We'll take it," he said, pulling out his wallet. "Does your price include shipping?"

"I'm sorry to say it doesn't. As you can imagine, shipping anything to and from Alaska is quite expensive, but I only charge you what the shipping company charges me. I'd be happy to e-mail you a copy of their invoice for your records."

"That will be fine," he said.

I rang up the sale, and they left the gallery happy. I knew the artist would be thrilled when she saw the price we'd settled on for the painting. She'd had a wonderful debut, and I was looking forward to a long and mutually beneficial partnership. After the couple left, I took down the painting and tucked it into my back room. I selected another painting from my shrinking stock and hurried back out to hang it, greeting a pair of women who were carrying telltale shopping bags from several of the shops that lined the harbor.

"Do you have any jewelry?" asked the younger of the two women.

"Yes, I have a charming line of jewelry handmade by a certified tribal artist who lives just outside town." I escorted them to the display case and left them admiring necklaces, rings, and broaches while I hung the painting and welcomed more customers into the gallery. Customers come in waves, flooding the shops as each new tender docks at the pier.

In Coho Bay, there were only two seasons that mattered—cruise ship and winter. Securing a spot on the cruising calendar had been the town's equivalent of winning the lottery. Each cruise line pays a fee to anchor offshore and ferry passengers to the town's refurbished dock. Shops like mine do enough business from May to September to carry us through the winter. I showcase the work of local artists, most of whom are native to southern Alaska. Since the ships started coming, a growing number of artists have been drawn here in search of backwoods inspiration. Many of them abandon Coho Bay when snow flies, but those who stay grow to cherish this coastline almost as much as those of us who were born here.

Cruise ship season is insanely busy. The first passengers arrive at the dock at eight in the morning and there is a steady flow of cruisers coming and going until the last tender leaves. We are one of the smallest ports on the Alaska tour, but one ship a day, six days a week, is more than enough business to satisfy us. Whether you own a shop or take cruisers on excursions in and around the bay, you're running all day long. On Thursdays, instead of relaxing, we all race to do the personal business that accumulates during the week. Nobody sleeps during cruise ship season, but we're not complaining. We get to meet people from all over the world who are always happy, because how can you not be happy on a cruise, and we all benefit from the economic windfall.

I was ringing up another sale and keeping an eye on the dozen or so customers who were drifting around the sales floor when I saw Taylor walk through the door. I dropped the credit card in my hand and had to duck under the sales counter to retrieve it. I swiped it three times before the reassuring message popped up on the screen to let me know the charge was processing. Thankfully my customer looked more amused than annoyed. "I'm so sorry. Sometimes the reader has a mind of its own."

That's right, Cara, I thought. *Throw the reader under the bus. It won't mind.* Somehow, I managed to complete the sale. I might even have remembered to thank her, but I wouldn't have bet on it.

Taylor was standing a few steps in from the entryway, looking at me with a bemused expression. I had only taken a few steps toward her when a customer called me over with a question about a watercolor. I smiled and shrugged at Taylor, who waved her hand at me. Customers came first, and she understood that. As I answered questions with half my brain, the other half buzzed with questions of my own, but there was no time to ask. It was late in the season, and my two assistants had gone back to school in Anchorage, leaving me swimming in a sea of customers. I knew she'd answer my questions eventually, but having to wait was sheer torture.

I sold the watercolor, then a small bronze casting of the enormous grizzly bear sculpture that graced the town square. The casting was my best-selling piece, with the proceeds going to Out of the Darkness, a charitable foundation which funded mental health services to help residents get through the long, dark Alaskan winters. The artist who created the sculpture had lost his own battle with depression, and his family had established the foundation in his memory.

By the time the bell on my door finally stopped ringing, Taylor had gone, but I knew where she'd be. I shoved the day's deposit into a bank bag and rushed out, locking the gallery behind me. I stopped dead when I caught sight of the sun sinking over the bay, deepening the shadows around me. My sister tells me that I should have a bumper sticker that says, *I brake for nature*. She's run me over more than a few times because I stopped suddenly to look at a flower or a tree or the way the mist rises from the water in the winter. I don't know why she gets mad. I'm the one with the bruises.

I breathed in the intoxicating mixture of sea salt, pine, and fresh-caught fish. Coho Bay was named for the salmon that had provided the majority of the town's income before the cruise ships. My parents had come here in the 1980s, craving a simple life close to nature. Bored by nature, as only a teenager can be, I had badgered them until they agreed to send me to college "outside," as Alaskans refer to the unfortunate other states. After one lonely year in Seattle, I had come home and finished my degree in Anchorage.

My urgency forgotten, I strolled along the wooden sidewalks that cruisers found so quaint. The old-timers had shaken their heads at the downtown merchants when we tore out the old cement sidewalks to install them, but they turned out to be surprisingly practical, standing up well to both the salt spray and wide swings in temperature. I passed the shuttered stores and outfitter shops, and stopped to drop my deposit into the night box at the bank. I crossed the road to Melody's Place, Coho Bay's only restaurant, smiling in anticipation of good food and lively conversation.

I pushed open the door and was engulfed in silence. Where there should have been a confused din of voices all trying to talk at once, each man and woman striving to tell a story funnier than the last, there was a deafening void. The tables were full, but the faces were grim. They stared up at me, some eyes questioning, some accusing. In classic Hollywood fashion, I spun around to see what they were looking at, but there was only me.

Snapping out of my shock, I walked into the crowded dining room and looked for Mel, who should have been bustling back and forth from the kitchen to the dining room. I found her, but there was no bustle. She was leaning against the back counter, as silent as her customers, surveying the room. Her face was stormy, but it relaxed when she saw me. She nodded toward the barstool that was my customary spot. Tonight it was occupied. Taylor. At least now I understood the silence.

Crossing the room, I greeted friends at every table I passed, bantering gently, nudging them back to life. My gesture had the desired effect, and by the time I reached the counter, there was a murmur of quiet conversation throughout the room. "Hey, Mel," I said with a cheer I didn't quite feel.

"Bent and I figured you'd want your dinner to go tonight." She handed me a plate wrapped in aluminum foil. Around that was a clean dish towel to keep the hot plate from burning me on the way home. I heard the room grow quiet again. I pictured a hundred eyes focused on me, a hundred ears attuned to the one conversation they were itching to hear.

"Yeah, thanks. Tay, you ready?" I took the plate, and as I did, Mel squeezed my hand.

"Thanks, Cara," she whispered.

Taylor slid off the stool, and I led her through the gauntlet. As we passed, fifty heads dropped and forks worked noisily. I knew the room would explode as soon as we were out of earshot, but let them get it out of their system. A little gossip added spice to life in a small town.

Taylor and I walked in silence until we reached the gallery. We turned to walk around the side of the rustic log building, and in spite of the million questions I was dying to ask her, my mind took a detour. Dad, Johnny, and I, with a little help from assorted friends and relatives, had built the gallery out of wood harvested from our own land and cut into beams and floorboards and cabinets at Lennon Millworks. It took months of backbreaking effort, a lot of laughter and a broken finger—Dad's, not mine—to turn the trees into a roomy gallery with an apartment upstairs. We weren't always sure we'd finish, but we'd roughed it in before snow flew, and by the time the first ship anchored offshore the following May, we had been ready. We weren't the most skillful builders on the bay, but every inch of that building carried pride of workmanship.

We'd made a great team, the three of us. Then Taylor had flown in from Seattle to help me get the gallery stocked for the first season and... well, that was three years ago. No sense in crying over spilt milk. I opened the door and promptly crashed into two oversized suitcases that were sitting in the entryway. "Cripes, Tay!" I grabbed one foot and hopped around on the other.

"Sorry. I didn't want to bother you, so I just popped these in on my way to Mel's."

"You could have taken them upstairs," I said, still hopping, which was quite a feat considering how small my entryway was and the fact that Taylor's suitcases were taking up most of it. "I think I broke my toe."

"Don't be so dramatic." She stepped gracefully over the small mountain of suitcases and started up the steps. "I'll bring them up later, that is, if you'll let me stay."

"Tay, you know you're always welcome here." I stopped hopping and gingerly put weight on my offending foot. It was sore, but it held, and I followed her a little less gracefully over the suitcases and up the steps. Those steps had been unexpectedly hard to build. Dad had put them in, torn them out, and put them in again twice before he declared that the uneven rise gave the place character. "I wish you'd let me know you were coming. I would have moved your renter into one of Dad's cabins."

"Who's at the house?"

"Mr. Peterson. You remember him."

"The writer?"

"The banker. He's the only one who thinks he's a writer." Mr. Peterson had been coming to Coho Bay for fifteen years, working on the novel he never seemed to finish. Sometimes he stayed in one of Dad's cabins, but he preferred the houses on the far side of the bay. "I knew you wouldn't want strangers living there, so when he asked about taking the house for the summer, I jumped. I'm heading out at the end of the season to get him. We can move you in at the same time."

Taylor nodded and wandered over to the tiny kitchen. "It's my own fault. I didn't know I was coming until I was here."

That was typical Taylor. "I don't have a guest room, but the couch is all yours. Unless you'd rather stay in one of the cabins. I have a couple empty right now."

Taylor made a face. "Running water?"

"When the catchment tank's full. Dad and I put composting toilets in over the winter though. Renters were complaining about having to use an outhouse, can you imagine?" I laughed at the look of horror on her face. Impulsively, I put my plate on the table and wrapped my arms around her. "I've missed you, Tay! I'm so glad you're back."

Taylor pulled away and walked across the room and stood looking out at the bay, where the sun was sending up flares of orange and red and gold. My father and I had put in a full wall of windows to take advantage of that view, and it was breathtaking. I only lived in the apartment during the season, but that view always tempted me to make it my home year-round. "I had no place else to go."

Her distress disturbed me, but I knew she'd only tell me what was bothering her when she was ready. The aroma of moose burger and onion rings made my mouth water, so I sat down to eat my dinner. Bent makes the absolute best burgers in town, and that's saying something in a town where most people make their own burgers from whatever meat they happen to have in the freezer. I've had burgers made from moose, deer, bear (don't try it), and even my namesake, caribou, but moose beats the others hands down. I love to hunt, and I love to eat, but there's no way even I could eat four or five hundred pounds of meat by myself. I give whatever I get to Bent, who expertly butchers it and keeps it in his home freezer. Hunting regulations prohibit him from serving wild game in the restaurant, but since I'm Mel's baby sister and he never charges me for my meals, he can feed me without breaking any rules.

I washed the plate in my tiny sink, even though I knew Bent would run it through the commercial dishwasher when I took it back, and put it on the counter with the towel folded neatly on top. I hadn't put much of a kitchen in the apartment since I hadn't expected to be cooking. I had a two-burner cooktop and a miniature refrigerator that matched the one I had in the back room of the gallery. A microwave oven and floor-to-ceiling pantry cabinet that held cereal, snacks and a few dishes, gave me everything I needed.

Taylor was sitting in a chair by the window, staring absently at the book in her hands, which she'd pulled off one of the bookcases that lined the apartment. Wherever there wasn't a window, there was a bookcase. I hadn't lived there long enough to have filled up more than a handful of the shelves, but everyone has a goal in life, and filling those shelves was one of mine.

"What'd you find?" I asked, switching on the light since the sun had set. She blinked, startled, and held up the book for me to see. "Oh, that's a good one. You'll enjoy it."

She nodded and went back to pretending to read the book. I sighed and picked up the one I was reading from where I'd left it the night before, face down on the coffee table. I hate to mistreat books that way, but I had been too tired to look for something to use as a bookmark. I get lost in books, especially when the days go on and on, and I don't realize how late it is until the light finally fades around midnight. It's September and the days are shorter, but now I read to kill time after dinner, and I still end up getting too little sleep. Mel keeps telling me I should get a boyfriend so I wouldn't have to spend my evenings buried in a book, but I'd never met a man who could live up to the ones in my complete set of Jane Austin novels.

Last Christmas Mom got me one of those electronic gizmos that people use to read books. She told me it was wasteful to kill trees for books, and I have to admit there was real appeal to being able to decide what I wanted to read, and after three seconds of downloading, be able to dive right in. Having books shipped to Coho Bay was prohibitively expensive, so I usually loaded up at the local bookstore whenever I took a trip into Juneau. Sometimes if there was a book I was dying to read, I'd ask Kenny, our mailman, to pick it up for me on one of his daily runs. I still have the reader, somewhere, but after the initial rush, I found I missed the sensory aspect of reading—the feel and the smell of the book and the sound of the pages turning. It's a funny thing, I know, and someday I'm sure the printed page will go the way of VHS tapes, but for me there's just nothing like holding a book in my hands.

Except that I couldn't concentrate tonight, any better than Taylor could, so she and I sat there in silence, both pretending to read, but both lost in our own thoughts. It took every bit of my admittedly small reserve of self-control to hold back the flood of questions that threatened whenever I looked up at her. Finally, I couldn't take it anymore. I stood up abruptly. "You must be exhausted, and here I am sitting on your bed. Why don't you get your suitcases, and I'll get out the spare bedding?"

"Are you sure? I don't want to put you out." A yawn almost split her face, and we both laughed.

"Go while you're still awake enough to make it back up the stairs." Taylor clomped down to the entryway, and I went to the bedroom to get the spare sheet and pillow I kept for the times when my parents came to visit. "The couch is comfortable," I said when she came back with one of her suitcases. "I sleep on it myself whenever my folks come over. I have a blanket too if you want one."

"No thanks," she said, shrugging her shoulders. "I'm always hot."

"Well, I'll put it on the chair in case you get cold in the middle of the night. You probably remember that I'm up and out early, but I'll try not to wake you. Sleep as late as you want, then come downstairs and keep me company."

"I could run the register for you."

"That would be amazing. You saw how crazy it gets, but go ahead and sleep in. The hoards won't show up before noon." That wasn't quite true, but Taylor had dark circles under her eyes that had never been there before. Whatever was troubling her, it would take more than one good night's rest to erase them.

"Cara?"

"Yes?"

"I..." Her face flushed. "Thank you."

"You're welcome, Tay. You're always welcome here." She turned away, and I thought it best not to press. I closed the door of my bedroom behind me and changed into an old flannel shirt. After brushing my hair and my teeth, I turned off the lights and crawled into bed. I expected to lay awake, wondering what had happened to Taylor and why she thought she had no place else to go, but I was asleep almost before my head hit the pillow.

Chapter 2

"It's four thirty, Cara."

"I know. I'm late. I'm sorry." I put the plate and dish towel on the stainless steel drain board and pulled an apron from the hooks where they hung by the door. Tying it on, I went to see what my sister was making. Mel was rolling out dough at the worktable. One industrial baking pan was already full and had been set aside.

"Reading?" Mel asked as she deftly covered the dough with cinnamon, sugar, raisins and chopped nuts, then rolled it into one long cinnamon log. She handed me a knife, and I sliced the dough into two-inch rolls and filled the second pan while Mel gathered up the dirty dishes and tossed them into the sink. "Or were you and Taylor up half the night gabbing?"

"I wish. She hasn't said a word."

"No! Seriously?" Mel went into the refrigerated storage room and brought out a flat of eggs, which she gently laid on the counter. "Did you know she was coming?"

"I would have told you."

Mel piled ingredients on the worktable and started making piecrust. "Why didn't she tell you she was coming? Didn't she know Mr. Peterson isn't leaving until the season ends? Where did she think she was going to stay?"

I slid the baking pan onto the rack so the rolls could rise and walked over to the sink. I washed my hands and let the water run until it was hot, then pushed down the stopper and let the water cascade over the dirty mixing dishes. I squeezed a generous dab of soap out and watched the suds rise. "All good questions but I don't have any answers."

"You didn't ask her? Hey, could you turn the oven on? Three seventy-five."

"I know. I wanted to ask, but you know how she gets."

"Yeah. Stubborn as a mule."

"And silent as the grave."

"Until she decides to talk and then—look out."

We both laughed, then went back to work. There was no time for small talk during the season. We had to make sure everything was ready before the first hungry local walked through the door. Mel was making quiche, and I started washing her baking dishes, our joint efforts giving Bent a chance to sleep for an extra hour. I could hear movement in their apartment, so I knew he'd be down soon. We'd all have breakfast in the kitchen, then I'd head to the gallery and they'd feed the horde of locals, rushing to eat before the first tender landed. It had been our routine for three seasons, and we had it down to a science.

"People sure seemed freaked out to see her," I said as I scrubbed.

Mel slid the quiche into the oven and set the timer before answering. "What'd you expect?" She dumped her dirty mixing bowl into the sink.

I sighed and fished it out of the water. "Always another bowl." I washed it and set it on the drying rack. "Tay must've hated everyone staring at her like that."

Mel snorted. "She had to have known how people would react. She didn't have to sit out in the dining room. She could have come around to the kitchen if she didn't want people staring at her."

"She's got too much pride to slink around. You know that, Mel, and I don't blame her. She doesn't have anything to apologize for."

"I agree, but that isn't gonna stop people from talking."

"It'll die down."

"Why would she want to come back here, Cara? I thought for sure she'd stay in Seattle."

"Who are we gossiping about today?" Mel and I exchanged guilty looks as Bent lumbered into the kitchen. I shrugged and started rinsing out the sink.

"You know perfectly well who." Mel's voice softened, her face flushed, and she couldn't keep from smiling. The way they carried on, you'd have thought they were newlyweds instead of closing in on their sixth anniversary.

"Why isn't she here for breakfast?" Bent laid his hand on my shoulder. "Hope she's not letting last night scare her away?"

"A few cold shoulders aren't gonna keep Tay away from your cooking. She's still asleep."

"City folk," said Bent, shaking his head in mock disgust. "Sleeping half the day away."

"I hope she does," I countered, matching his playful tone. "She was dead on her feet last night. I get the feeling she hasn't been sleeping much lately."

"Something did seem to be bothering her when she came in," agreed Mel. "Didn't seem like herself at all. I had to look twice to make sure it was her."

"Whatever it is, it must be pretty bad to drive her back here after everything that happened."

"Feels like a sausage day, don't you think, ladies?" asked Bent, cutting off our speculations and drawing us back to the work at hand.

"You goof," said Mel, swatting mildly at him. He ducked away, his laughter filling the kitchen as he lumbered off to the storage room.

He returned, his arms full of supplies, singing a bawdy bar song in a slightly off-key baritone. When there were customers in the dining area, Bent resigned himself to whistling along with the radio, but when it was just family, he would cut loose with songs he'd picked up in the Navy. At first I'd found his lyrics quite shocking, but as I'd gotten to know him better, I'd started to sing along with him, inserting nonsense words for the ones that made me blush. Bent found this highly amusing and sometimes sang my lyrics instead of his. The sight of this bear of a man belting out G-rated bar songs sent Mel into fits of laughter.

After breakfast, I headed off with a promise of leftover quiche for lunch. I hurried up the boardwalk that ran along the harbor, enjoying the predawn quiet. The lights of today's cruise ship, which was anchored in deep water, reminded me that this boardwalk wouldn't be quiet long and I still had a lot of work to do. Reaching city hall, I looked up at the gallery and treated myself to a moment of proprietary pride. The Broken Antler Gallery was my own brainchild, a way to put my business education to good use while giving local artists an outlet for their work. The log cabin construction reflected the carefully cultivated rustic style chosen by the merchants to appeal to the tourists. I unlocked the front door and slipped in, locking it behind me. I threaded my way through the gallery, moving from memory since it was too dark to see. I had two hours before dawn broke and another hour before the first tender would arrive. That should be plenty of time to get caught up on the paperwork I never had time to do while the gallery was open.

I flipped on the light in the back room and started coffee. Steaming mug in hand, I fired up my computer and started going through yesterday's sales. Methodically, I went through each transaction, making sure that every sale was credited to the correct artist and printing out labels for the pieces that needed to be shipped. I keep thirty-five percent of each sale as my commission, making my gallery wildly popular with artists all over the region. Most art dealers take a substantially bigger cut, some as much as sixty percent of the sale. Because my family owned the land outright and my father and I had harvested the materials and contributed most of the labor, my overhead was very low. I could afford to operate on less commission and still earn a profit. This enabled me to attract artists even during my first season in business. The Broken Antler Gallery quickly developed a reputation for carrying the best work by the best artists in southern Alaska, earning both my artists and me a good living.

One by one, I carefully packaged the previous day's artwork. Art is fragile and needs careful crating to safely make the journey from Coho Bay to buyers around the world. When Coho Bay won our contract with the first cruise ship line, it took two years before the initial ship sailed into the bay. I'd bartered with a gallery in Juneau, providing them free labor for a season in exchange for being able to learn the nuts and bolts of the business. It saved me years of trial and error. I was just putting the label on the last box when the doorbell rang. I switched on the lights in the gallery and went to open the door. "Morning, Kenny."

Kenny had been running the mail between Juneau and Coho Bay as long as anyone could remember. He'd been old when I was a girl, but even though I had aged, he never seemed to change. He wore an old leather bomber jacket and had a collection of baseball caps, some advertising local businesses and some with pithy sayings. Today's read, *Wishin' I was Fishin'* and had a small picture of a man fishing out of the back of a rowboat.

"Mornin,' Cara. Whatcha got for me?"

We spent the next few minutes shuttling crates and cartons through the store and out to his truck. Every morning Kenny went all over town gathering the mail and packages. He loaded them onto his boat and ran them up to Juneau. There he'd exchange the outgoing for the incoming and make the return trip to Coho Bay. He'd make his delivery rounds in the afternoon, providing daily service during the season and twice a week, weather permitting, through the winter. The whole town shared a single address—Rural Route One—but Kenny knew where everyone lived.

After he left, I stood in the doorway, looking out at the bay. The sun was rising over the mountains behind me, bathing the cruise ship in soft golden light. The season always passes in a blur, and it was hard to believe it was nearly over. Two ships after this one, and it would be time to shift into winter mode. I watched the sky lighten, soaking in the quiet beauty of early morning and waving to the trickle of locals who passed by, heading for their stores or excursion boats. Watching the sunrise over the bay never left me feeling anything but awe even after twenty-six years of sunrises. This simple but staggering beauty was what anchored me to Alaska. I was as much a part of the alchemy of the state as the trees and the rivers and the bears.

A long, low horn sounded from the cruise ship, cutting through my reverie and reminding me I had to restock before the first tender docked. I could see it pulling alongside the ship to take on the first wave of passengers. In half an hour, the first fifty passengers would pour out of the tender onto the dock and into the town. I tore myself away from the sunrise and started pulling artwork from the storage room to fill empty spaces. By the time the bell jingled on the gallery door, I was ready.

"Do you have any Jonathan Snow? I've been asking at every stop on this cruise, and I hear you're the only gallery that carries his work."

I looked at the woman who'd asked the question, wondering whether she was a serious collector or just another gawker. "Yes, Snow grew up in Coho Bay."

"Then I'm not too late?" She was breathless, but I still wasn't sure whether her eagerness was because of the art or the artist. Tabloids and cable news had been full of lurid stories after Johnny's death, and the demand for his work had far outpaced the supply, driving the prices through the roof. An artist's work usually increases in value after his or her death, but I'd never seen anything like the feeding frenzy that hit after Johnny died.

"I have two of his paintings left." I led her to the back of the gallery where the stunning oils were displayed. "As you can imagine, there's been quite a demand for his work."

She sighed when she caught sight of the paintings. Her features took on a look I'd seen many times, when someone who truly appreciates art sees a piece that speaks to her soul. *Collector*, I decided. Johnny would have been pleased by her reaction, even though it was unlikely she would be able to afford to buy. He had always been more interested in the emotional impact of his art than the financial.

"Do you mind if I…" Her voice fell away.

"Of course not. Please take all the time you want." I left her there and returned to the counter in time to see

Taylor come through the gallery doors. She was dressed in a white T-shirt under a burgundy, button-down shirt over neatly pressed tan pants. The Merchant's Association had settled on this look during our first season. Each business chose a different shirt color, and I had chosen a deep burgundy for the gallery. Taylor's was probably the same outfit she'd worn when she used to work with me. It had been thoughtful of her not only to save it after she'd gotten married, but to bring it with her. Still, if she'd thought ahead enough to pack the outfit, it was odd she hadn't thought to let me know she was coming. Well, that was Taylor, never quite crossing the *t*'s or dotting the *i*'s.

"Morning," she said, sliding behind the counter.

"Afternoon. Sleep well?"

Taylor leaned over to look at the clock on the counter, carefully hidden from customer view. Clocks made cruisers hurry, worried they'd miss the last tender back to the ship, so you won't find one on display in any of our shops. She blushed. "Sorry. Jet lag."

"You flew in from Seattle, Tay. That's only one time zone. At least you've stopped looking like something the cat dragged in."

She turned her back to the sales floor and stuck her tongue out at me. Turning back, her eyes moved slowly around the room until they rested on the woman who was admiring Johnny's work. A man with a camera had joined her. "That all you have left?" he called out.

"Yes. You know how it is when an artist..." I stopped, suddenly self-conscious.

"Dies. I know," said Tay. I could feel my face redden. "Stop it, Cara. You're the one person I thought I could trust not to treat me with kid gloves."

"Nobody was treating you with kid gloves last night."

Taylor's eyes took on a guarded look, and I kicked myself. I have got to stop saying the first thing that comes into my head. To my surprise, she giggled. "It was like being in a cheesy movie. I walked through the door and wham! Silence. I almost laughed." She shook her head, her smile fading. "Then it wasn't funny anymore."

"They were surprised to see you, that's all. So was I. I wish you'd let me know you were coming."

"So they could pretend to be happy to see me? What's the point?"

We put our conversation on hold as the man with the camera approached. "May I help you find something, sir?"

"I'm interested in those Snow paintings you have. What are you asking?" I named a price, and he raised an eyebrow.

"Negotiable?"

"I'm afraid not. There are several museums inquiring about his work, and these are the only pieces I have left."

There was silence as we each waited for the other to speak. In negotiations, breaking the silence signals to the other player that you want the deal more than they do, giving them the upper hand. It's a ridiculous game, but one I had learned to play well. He pulled a business card out of his pocket and handed it to me. "I may have a buyer for you. I'll have to consult my client and let you know."

"That would be fine. Here's my card. Feel free to call me if you have any questions."

He looked at the card. "Caribou King. That can't possibly be your real name."

"It is indeed. I was born in a log cabin about five miles from here."

He slid the card into his shirt pocket. "I like it. Real Alaska. I'll let you know what my buyer says."

After he left, Taylor put her head against mine and whispered, "Good thing you didn't deck him for making fun of your name."

I stifled a laugh because the gallery was full of customers. "Good thing he doesn't know those museums wanted me to donate Johnny's paintings."

Taylor giggled. "Hey, you just said they'd inquired, not that they'd flashed any cash."

"Exactly." We fell into a familiar and comfortable rhythm, me walking the gallery floor, talking to the customers, Taylor working the register and answering an unending stream of tourist questions. When I'd opened The Broken Antler three years ago, Taylor had come up from Seattle to help. She'd fallen in love with a shy young artist named John Lennon. Johnny had been my best friend since grade school, and I'd been working up my nerve to tell him I wanted to be more than friends, but it was clear once he met her that Johnny had fallen hard. It was Taylor who suggested his professional name—Jonathan Snow—and it was that name she'd agreed to take when he'd proposed.

Midafternoon brought a lull, so I left Taylor in charge and hurried to Mel's. After a month of working alone from dawn until dark, it was lovely to be walking down the boardwalk in daylight. Mel disappeared into the kitchen as I came in, so I waited for her at the counter. I stood since my barstool was occupied.

"Sorry, Boo. Want me to move?" Frank Baker was an odd combination of annoying and—no, come to think of it, he was annoying with a side of even more annoying.

"Stop calling me that."

"Oh, come on, it's cute."

"Can I call you Hot Dog? Would that be cute?"

"Aw heck, Cara. You take all my fun away."

"You shouldn't be having fun in the middle of the day. You should be out on the bay with a boat full of tourists. What happened?" Frank ran excursions, taking cruisers whale watching, salmon fishing, and on bay tours. I'd heard enough of my customers talk about his tours to know he was good at what he did, and his tours were always full.

"Whales have all gone south. Only doing bay tours now. You're the one who shouldn't be here. Don't you have a gallery to run?"

Mel came back with my lunch, and I thanked her. "See you, Frank."

"Walk you back?"

"You know, Frank, I might actually like you if you were normal all the time instead of acting like an overgrown frat boy."

"Where's the fun in that?" he laughed.

I liked the sound of his laughter, but there was no time for that kind of fun during cruise ship season. I waved to Mel and headed back out the door. Frank was a good-looking single man of my age, and that was as rare as diamonds in Coho Bay. He'd been flirting with me all summer, but I had a feeling those days were about to be over. He'd meet Taylor tonight, and he wouldn't be the first man who lost all interest in flirting with me once he laid eyes on her.

Another single man was waiting for me at the door to the gallery, only I was pretty sure Coho Bay's one and only policeman hadn't come to flirt. "Hello, Dan. What brings you here today?"

"Heard Taylor Lennon was back in town. Figured she'd be here."

"Taylor Snow," I corrected.

Dan made a face. He'd never approved of Johnny calling himself by anything other than his given name, so he'd called him Lennon until the day he died. It hadn't bothered Johnny, but it had bothered Taylor, something that tickled Dan since he'd never liked her. Judging by the look on her face when he followed me inside, I'd say the feeling was mutual.

"Taylor, you remember Dan Simmons." She nodded her head but didn't speak. I put the two plates of quiche on the counter, hidden from customer view. "Dan, what can we do for you?"

Dan glowered at Taylor until she broke eye contact. "I'm wondering if I might talk to Ms. Lennon."

Taylor's eyes snapped back to his, and her chin went up. "It's Snow. What do you want?"

"Just want to ask you a few questions."

"About what?"

My customers had stopped looking at art and were instead watching the scene at the counter. "Dan, can't this wait?"

"Sorry, Cara. I'll come back later." Dan knew better than to air dirty laundry in front of customers. Whatever he needed to ask Taylor, he knew it took a backseat to providing a warm and welcoming environment for our guests.

"Let's get it over with." Taylor held the back room door open and gestured to Dan. "We can talk in here."

"Keep your voice down," I whispered to Dan as he passed me.

They disappeared into the back room, and I heard the muffled sound of voices but nothing distinct. I looked around the gallery and faces turned away from me as customers pretended they hadn't noticed the local police take what appeared to be one of my employees into the back room for questioning. The door jingled a little more briskly than usual as potential sales evaporated. To spend thousands of dollars for a work of art, a buyer must trust the seller, so any hint of scandal kills sales. Dan knew that, and I fumed that he'd come to the gallery during business hours when he could easily have talked to Taylor after the last tender left.

Stifling my anger, I promised myself I would let Dan know exactly what I thought of him as soon as I could corner him at Mel's. I popped a forkful of quiche into my mouth and felt my eyes roll back in my head at the melt-in-your-mouth pastry. Mel's quiche can make a girl forget just about any trouble, and I gave myself up to the enjoyment of my food. I should have been circulating on the floor, talking about paintings and sculptures, calming any qualms about what the police might be doing in the gallery, but I had a feeling it was too late for this crowd and I wouldn't be attracting buyers again until Dan was gone. The gallery emptied, with more than a few curious glances at the back room door as the might-have-been customers left.

With an empty gallery and an empty plate, I looked at Taylor's untasted quiche and hoped she'd have an appetite for it. Taylor was fidgety when it came to food. My ability to eat almost anything and retain my bean-pole figure was one of only two things Taylor had ever told me she envied about me—my metabolism and my rock-solid relationship with my parents and Mel. Taylor had lost her parents and her only brother in a plane crash when she was fifteen years old. She'd been at a prep school back east, and they'd been flying out to spend Thanksgiving with her. I hadn't known her then, but I knew all these years later she still grieved. When she'd first come to Coho Bay, my family had embraced her, and she'd told me it was the first time she felt she belonged since she'd lost her family.

I squirmed in my chair and checked the clock. Twenty-two minutes. What could they possibly be talking about for twenty-two minutes? It couldn't be about Johnny's death since that had been an accident.

His body had been found by a pair of hikers at the base of a drop-off below one of the trails Johnny had loved to wander, sketchpad beside him, as if ready to capture a flower or vista that awakened his imagination. Bears generally avoid populated areas during the summer, but in spring and fall, they come closer to town seeking food. To live in harmony with nature in bear country, we use locked, reinforced metal trash bins and we don't put out food for birds or squirrels since the feeders will attract bears. I don't exactly fear bears, but I have a very healthy respect for them and the danger they present. A bear will charge you if it feels threatened, and that must have been what happened to Johnny. He should have known better than to let his guard down on that trail. But for all his strengths, Johnny had been prone to lose himself in his surroundings, and that afternoon he had paid for his carelessness with his life.

Twenty-nine minutes and the bell on the gallery door jingled. I smiled, walking around the counter to greet the couple. At least this pair wouldn't have concerns about why the police were here. I was standing with them ten minutes later, discussing a bronze sculpture of a moose, when Dan walked out of the back room. He nodded at me as he passed, but his expression was unreadable. I looked to see if Taylor followed him, but the counter area was vacant.

"I'll just leave you to discuss your impressions of the works we've seen," I said to the couple. "You let me know if you have any questions." Deliberately keeping my steps unrushed to prevent the prospective buyers from thinking something might be wrong, I went to check on her.

She was sitting on my leather love seat and looked up with red-rimmed eyes when I came in, her makeup streaking across her face. I had only taken a step toward her when I heard the woman call to me from the gallery. "Go," said Taylor. "I'll be okay in a minute."

I returned to the sales floor and found the couple ready to discuss price. Some people assume an art dealer would prefer customers know very little about art, thinking that those customers will overpay, enriching both dealer and artist. That might be true for a few unscrupulous dealers, but for me it's just the opposite. I love to negotiate with customers who are at least as knowledgeable as I am because they know the value of what they are buying and are willing to pay a fair price. Customers with limited knowledge have no idea why works are priced at a certain level. To accommodate buyers who simply want something pretty and affordable, I try to showcase one or two emerging artists every season. This couple, who had an extensive collection back home in Germany, were a delight to negotiate with, and thirty minutes later, both customers and dealer came away satisfied. If all of my customers were like this couple, I'd be a happy girl.

As I spoke with the German couple, more cruisers trickled in, and before long, the gallery was bustling again. Taylor came out to work the counter without a hint of her earlier distress. "We'll talk later," she said, pushing me onto the sales floor while she ate her quiche as if she hadn't seen food in days.

I was dying to know what Dan had said to her that made her cry, but this was no time for a serious discussion. I plastered a smile onto my face and held my arms open. "Welcome to The Broken Antler Gallery, folks. Please let me know if you have any questions."

"How come you call it broken antler?" asked a boy who appeared to be about seven or eight years old.

His mother tried to shush him, but I smiled warmly and crouched down to meet him at eye level. I pointed at a set of elk antlers mounted on the wall behind the counter. One side was glorious, but the other was broken off about three-quarters of the way up. "Do you see those antlers?"

The boy nodded. "They ain't real."

"They certainly are real. They're from the elk I got when I went on my very first elk hunt. I wasn't much bigger than you."

He made a sour face. "Girls don't hunt."

"Some girls don't, but some girls do. We hunt up here or we don't eat."

"But antlers don't look like that."

"Honey, let's let the nice lady run her gallery," said the boy's mother, her face red with embarrassment.

I smiled reassuringly at her. "He's okay. I love curiosity; it inspires creative minds." I turned my attention back to the boy. "Usually antlers will be pretty much the same on both sides, but this elk had broken off one side of his, probably in a fight with another elk over a lady elk."

"Girls," said the boy with a look of disgust. "That figures."

Chapter 3

Every head turned when Taylor walked into Mel's with me, but the shock from last night had passed, so the noise level only took a momentary dip. When we came in, Mel bumped Frank from a barstool to a table, where he settled into conversation with some seasonal guides. Frank had only been in Coho Bay for a year, so he hadn't yet earned "butt rights" as Mel called the preference locals had for sitting in the exact same place night after night. Taylor only slightly outranked him, but she was with me and that would have overruled him if he'd voiced any objections.

I watched Frank's face closely as he caught sight of Taylor. His eyes moved slowly down her body, as though caressing her, and my heart sank. I'd seen that look before, in the eyes of guys I was dating when they'd met her, and Frank and I hadn't even gone out yet. There was definitely desire in that look, and a hint of something beneath the desire that I couldn't quite define. Not that I blamed him. Taylor was a dazzling blond pixie who somehow managed to make the simple "uniform" look like she'd been dressed by a designer. Standing next to her, I suddenly felt awkward and overgrown. I stood a good foot taller, and where her figure curved in all the right places, mine barely broke the surface.

I caught sight of Dan, who was sitting at his regular table by the front window. His eyes were also fixed on Taylor, but the heat that rose from his gaze was not sexual. At least there was one unmarried man in town immune to her charms. Immune to mine too, if I had any charms. In the years he'd been in Coho Bay, Dan had never spared a second glance at me, and frankly I had never found him too appealing either. Dan was shorter than me and stocky with the body of a wrestler. He had a buzz cut and never grew a beard, not even when most men sprouted facial hair to combat the cold. It struck me that I didn't know very much about Dan. He'd spent summers here with his uncle, who'd been chief of police, but our paths had rarely crossed. Dan had been the natural choice for the job when his uncle had retired, but even after he moved here, I hadn't made an effort to get to know him. If I were going to lose what little chance I'd had with Frank to Taylor, I might have to push myself to give Dan another look.

It was a depressing thought. Maybe love and marriage were overrated. After all, I was happy with my life just the way it was. Could having a man in my life make it any better than it was now? My mother had thought so. It hadn't taken her six months after Mel and Bent got married before she'd started "noticing" eligible bachelors and pointing them out to me. Fortunately, since single men were few and far between, she'd had limited opportunities to embarrass me.

Bent rarely served salmon to the locals. Everyone in Coho Bay had a freezer full of salmon, and all winter long we'd eat so much wild game and frozen or smoked salmon that by summer we couldn't stand the thought of it. The cruisers loved Alaskan salmon though, so Bent always kept some on hand. Nobody makes salmon as well as he does, so I was always happy when he made a little too much for the lunch crowd and it spilled over into dinner. When Mel slid the plate in front of me, all thoughts of men and marriage vanished, and Bent's heavenly salmon filet was all that mattered.

Taylor didn't like salmon, which to me was like not liking air or water, but it was a free country. If she wanted to eat salad instead of salmon, who was I to call her out on it?

We were splitting a leftover cinnamon roll when the room went silent behind us. I spun around on my stool. "Crap." I spoke quietly so only Taylor heard me. She turned to look, and the expletive she uttered was a little bit stronger than mine had been.

A man in his fifties, sleeves rolled up on his flannel shirt, revealing muscular arms earned the old-fashioned way by felling logs and putting them through his lumber mill. Cruise ships hadn't changed Jack Lennon's life. Johnny's father was always busy during the season since any building that needed to be done had to be done during the long, warm days of the summer. They had been as far apart in personality as it was possible for a father and son to be, but when Johnny's mother had died, they'd been forced to find ways to bridge the gap between them. Johnny embraced the artistic side of his father's business, building furniture and cabinets while Jack turned out planks and shaved logs for construction. They'd grown thick as thieves until Taylor had swept into Johnny's life. One look at her, and Johnny lost interest in sawdust and boards.

"I heard you were back." The steel in Jack's tone sent sparks through the room.

I slid off my stool and stood in front of Taylor. "Evening, Mr. Lennon," I said, fighting to keep my voice calm. Jack had been furious when Johnny died, blaming Taylor for his death. The fact that Johnny had been walking in a known bear area without bells, bear spray, or a firearm hadn't mattered to him.

Jack spared a brief look at me. "Hidin' behind Caribou's skirts ain't gonna help ya. I thought ya had more sense than to show yer face around here again."

I shot a pointed look at the table by the window. Dan rolled his eyes, but he got up, his chair scraping loudly. Jack turned to look at him. "Sit yer fat ass back down, Dan. Ya call yerself the law?" Jack spit onto the floor, causing Kenny, who'd been sitting nearby, to pull his feet away and glare up at Jack. Jack looked startled. "Sorry, Ken."

"No problem," said Kenny, a shake in his voice. The two men were about the same age, but Jack had at least forty pounds of muscle on Kenny. Jack was normally an affable sort, but when he'd been drinking, he could be downright nasty.

Jack turned his attention back to Dan, who had moved within a few feet of him. "She killed m'boy, Dan. Everbuddy knows it."

"Simmer down, Jack, that's the beer talking." Dan's voice was firm but friendly, seeking to calm the older man, who was a good bit taller and stronger. Not taking my eyes off them, I pulled Taylor off her barstool and edged her toward the kitchen.

Jack spat again and again. He had to apologize to Kenny, who moved his chair as far away as he could without hitting the next table. "Hell, Dan, don't gimme that crap." His voice took on a high-pitched, sing-song tone. "*I cain't arrest her. There ain't no evidence.* Ya'd have plenty of evidence if ya'd just git off yer ass and look fer it!"

In a small town, everyone knows everyone else's sore spots, and we all knew Dan hated any insult to his physique. Combine that with a slur to his law enforcement abilities, and it was no wonder his face turned as red as it did. Dan may have gotten his job through family ties, but he wasn't without credentials.

He'd been a detective in Anchorage before coming to Coho Bay, quite a coup for a man in his early thirties. When tourists treated him like a hick, all he could do was smile and nod at them, but I'd seen him punch a local man for less than what Jack had just said. "You watch your mouth, Jack. Nobody wants to listen to a drunken fool. You get outta here before I run you in."

"Oh, ya would arrest me fer speakin' the truth, but her," he gestured to Taylor, "you let her run around all she wants after killin' my boy."

Dan put a hand on Jack's arm, but he shrugged it off. I think he might have taken a swing at Dan if Frank hadn't stepped between them. A foot taller than the two other men, he was surprisingly muscled, a fair rival to Jack's bulging arms. How had I not noticed that? Frank's voice carried an authority I'd never heard from him before. I felt the heat rise on my face and wondered where this side of Frank had been hiding all summer.

"I'll walk you home, Mr. Lennon," he said to Jack. "I've been wanting to see that table you told me about. The one you built from a tree that got hit by lightning."

Jack stood for a moment, his eyes blinking up at Frank as though he didn't know who he was. I held my breath and got ready to run, but I needn't have worried. Apparently thinking better of starting a fight with Frank, Jack shoved Dan out of his way and headed out the door. Dan and Frank exchanged looks, then grabbed their coats and trailed out after him. Before the door even stopped swinging, the room burst with excited conversation. The crisis over, I leaned back against the counter and started to shake.

"Never dull around here," said Mel. She was standing next to Taylor, shotgun in hand. I don't think the men had even glanced her way during their standoff.

"You coulda said something so I'd known you had my back."

She smiled. "Always, little sister. I shouldn't have to tell you that."

"You people are nuts," said Taylor, coming out from the counter and climbing back onto her barstool.

"Why thank you," said Mel, returning to the kitchen. The fact that Bent had let her come out without him was proof enough of how badly I'd overreacted. My pulse began to return to normal.

"She ever actually shoot anybody?" asked Taylor.

"Not that I know of." I climbed onto my own stool. "Did you get a load of the muscles on Frank? When did that happen?"

Taylor tilted her head at me. "What rock have you been under?"

"So sue me. I never noticed."

"Mel says you've been flirting with him all summer."

"I have not!"

"Hey, don't shoot the messenger. Besides, I don't blame you. I could go for him myself."

Something in the pit of my stomach turned. Taylor is my friend, maybe my best friend, but she's not always easy to love. If she's attracted to a man, she sleeps with him, just like that. When she turned twenty-one, she had a different man in her bed every night for a week. She'd called me a prude, but a week of wishing we had thicker walls in our apartment had not been my idea of a good time. More than once she'd slept with a guy she knew I had my eye on. Any guy who'd jump into bed with Taylor wasn't the guy for me, but that didn't excuse her behavior. There was nothing between Frank and me, but I still didn't like the idea of her moving in on him.

"Get your own guy," I told her.

"Come on, Cara. Get in the game. You like him and he likes you. Why aren't you sleeping with him?"

"Tay!"

"You're twenty-six years old. What are you waiting for?"

"Cara, are you all right? Your face is red." I don't know when Mel had come in from the kitchen, but from the grin on her face, I'd say she'd heard most of the conversation. I stuck my tongue out at her, and she laughed and passed through to the dining room, coffeepot in hand.

I'd lost my appetite, so I pushed the plate toward Taylor. "I'm sorry about Jack."

"You're not doing yourself any favors waiting for him to make the first move," Tay continued, ignoring me. "A guy needs to know he's not gonna strike out, or he won't even try."

"Jack," I repeated, ignoring her. I was not in the mood to defend my values.

"Have it your way." She picked up her fork. "I feel sorry for Jack. I'm sure my coming back has stirred things up for him. Losing Johnny like that..." She shuddered. "After he'd lost his wife, it's enough to drive a man out of his mind."

"I suppose so, but he shouldn't go around saying you killed Johnny. That's crazy."

"He's been saying it since the day Johnny died. He's not going to stop now."

"Nobody killed Johnny. It was horrible but it wasn't murder."

"Maybe it's easier for him to have someone to blame."

"I don't see *you* blaming anybody."

Taylor pushed what was left of the roll around her plate with her fork. "I blame myself."

"Tay—"

"No, Cara. Let's not talk about it, okay?"

Memories of that grim day stole in like the fog creeping over the bay. Johnny's death would be exactly a year ago on Saturday. I didn't know much about grief, but anniversaries were supposed to be hard on people. Maybe that was why Taylor had come back when she did. They'd only been married a couple of years, but they'd been inseparable during that time. The only time anyone would see them apart was when Johnny felt "the call of the woods" as he called it. When that happened, Johnny would take off with his sketchpad, and she would busy herself at their island home or, as she had on that day, come into town and visit me at the gallery.

The whole town had turned out that evening to watch Dan bring Johnny's body down to the dock. Since he'd already been dead by the time he was found, there had been no urgency, and Dan had waited until the last tender left before calling in the state police boat that would take Johnny's body for autopsy in Juneau. I'd stood on the dock with my arms around Taylor, who'd been sobbing since she'd heard the news.

She'd thrown herself across Johnny's lifeless chest, and the crowd had stood by in silent sympathy. Then Jack had pushed his way through. "Get away from m'boy!" he'd shouted, grabbing Taylor's arm and yanking her away from the body. It had been a heart-wrenching sight. Only after the state police had threatened to arrest him had Jack allowed Dan to take him home. I had stood on the dock with Taylor, watching with her until the boat disappeared, pushing away my own pain to be strong for her. I'd known Johnny since grade school, but while there'd been some heat between us, we'd never been more than friends.

"You can make allowances for him if you want," said Mel, coming to trade her empty pot for a full one, "but he was out of line then and he's out of line now."

"Let me help," I said, sliding off the stool. At every table I visited, the questions were many but the answers few. Nobody defended Taylor, her being an outsider, but neither could they bring themselves to defend Jack's behavior. People felt bad for him, but whether they liked her or not, they just couldn't blame Taylor for the bear attack that had killed her husband.

There was a knock at my door that night. I was engrossed in a thriller—always a mistake in a quiet house on a dark night—and the sound startled me into dropping my book. "Crap," I said, flipping through the crimped pages but not finding the one I'd been reading. From the way my heart was pounding, maybe that was for the best. I dropped the book on the table and went downstairs. The next day was Thursday, the one day in the week where there were no cruise ships, so the whole town took the day off. I had given Taylor my bedroom because there was still far too much darkness in the circles beneath her eyes. She needed sleep and as much of it as she could get. As was my habit on Wednesday nights, I would be up half the night reading anyway, and on those nights, I often fell asleep on the couch even when I had the place to myself.

I went down the steps, finding my visitor already standing in the entryway. "You should lock your door."

"I never lock my door. Do you want to come up, Frank?" I stood back, and he walked past me and started up the stairs. I went to the door and poked my head out. There were a few porch lights, nothing out of the ordinary, but somehow tonight the shadows seemed menacing. I shook my head, dismissing the sense of foreboding. I have got to stop reading scary books late at night. I locked the door and padded up the stairs.

Frank was standing in the kitchen, his hands on his hips, waiting for me. When I reached the top of the stairs, he crossed to the window and looked down onto the road. "Don't you have curtains?"

"Did you come here in the middle of the night to criticize my decorating?"

He stepped back. Switching off the lamp, he joined me in the kitchen where the light over the sink cast a dim glow. "Just worried about your safety. Yours and your friend's. Where is she?"

"Sleeping. Why are you suddenly concerned about my safety?" He raised one eyebrow and looked down at me. An electric charge ran through my body, and I took a step back, bumping into the counter. How had I never noticed he was so tall?

"Asks the woman whose sister had to pull out a shotgun today."

So he had noticed. "Jack was drunk. Tay's coming back set him off. He'll calm down now he's got it out of his system. Can I get you a drink?" I pulled a carton of milk out of the fridge and reached into the cupboard for a glass.

A lopsided grin stole across his face. "Need to see ID for that?"

"Nah, it's low fat. None of the hard stuff for me."

He took the glass I handed him. "He was swearing a blue streak all the way home. Took both of us to get him inside."

"You didn't leave Dan alone with him, did you?"

"Simmons left when I did, why?"

"Jack hates Dan. Has since long before Johnny died."

"Simmons seems decent enough. Lennon got a reason?"

"Dan's uncle was chief of police when I was a kid. When he retired, word is Jack lobbied for Johnny to get the job, but Johnny didn't want it. The city hired Dan instead."

"Word is? Don't you know?"

"I was away at college when it happened."

"If his son didn't want the job, why does Lennon hold it against Simmons? Doesn't like outsiders?"

"Dan's not an outsider, he's from Homer. Jack just wants what he wants, is all. He doesn't take no for an answer."

"What did he think of his son being an artist? That couldn't have set well with him."

I drank my milk, wondering why Frank was suddenly so interested. There'd been some epic battles between the two, but Johnny had followed his heart and Jack had fallen into a bottle. He'd gotten ripping drunk at Johnny's wedding and the rift had only partially mended. "Maybe guilt is part of why Jack drinks. Something changed in him when Johnny died."

Frank wandered around my apartment, stopping to look at my books, though it was too dark for him to read the titles on the spines. "Probably doesn't like me," he said at last.

"Don't take it personally." I stood, watching him. There was something about him tonight so different from the lighthearted, easygoing man he'd always seemed to be. I am intense by nature, in almost everything I do, and it's hard for me to picture myself going through life as breezily as Frank. Tonight I was seeing a serious side to him, and I had to admit I found it appealing. There was something about him that made me feel safe. Maybe it was just the late hour and maybe I was more tired than I realized because my thoughts weren't making much sense even to me.

Frank paused at the window, and I saw his body tense. He ducked to one side and peered out, his face masked in the shadows.

"What is it?" He motioned for me to join him but pushed me behind him. Suddenly not feeling safe, I peered over his shoulder. "What are we looking at?"

"Wait for it," he said, still staring at the street.

There was nothing there. No lights, no people, no movement except the leaves that were bumping down the street in the wind. "I don't see anything," I whispered when I couldn't be quiet any longer.

"It's gone now—wait, there! Did you see that?"

I looked intently in the direction he was pointing, wondering if he were pulling my leg, when I saw it too. There was someone there, standing in the shadows, hidden by the awning of the building across the street. I stepped back, banging my shoulder into a bookcase. I rubbed the sore spot. "Who would be out this late?"

"Can't be Lennon. He was passed out cold when I left." Frank looked again. "Could be Simmons. That's the city office building, isn't it?"

"Yes, but wouldn't he have gone home?"

"Maybe he was worried about you too."

I stopped whispering and took another step back, careful to avoid the bookcase this time. "I'm fine. Except for strange men coming around in the middle of the night scaring me half to death."

Frank was still looking out the window. "I don't think he's trying to scare you. He probably doesn't know you've seen him."

"I wasn't talking about him."

Frank turned to look at me. "I'm just trying to help."

"Then tell Mr. Shoes down there to go home and go to bed. Then you do the same."

"You have a gun for protection?"

"Of course."

"Good. Lock the door behind me."

"If I promise to do that, will you get out of here so I can get some sleep?"

"If that's what you want." He looked down at me with an expression I didn't recognize, but I felt my body respond to it. I didn't think it was the sudden scare causing this tingling.

"Let's go then." I followed him down the stairs and locked the door behind him. I locked the deadbolt for good measure and went back upstairs. Out of curiosity, I went to the window and looked down at the city building. There were two sets of shoes visible now. Apparently Mr. Shoes wasn't dangerous, because neither set of feet appeared to be in a hurry to move on.

"What was that all about?" I asked the bookcase beside me. Bookcases not being inclined to tell you what they might be thinking, I turned off the light in the kitchen and settled myself on the couch. I fell asleep wondering whether I liked the new, heroic Frank more than I had the old, comfortable one.

Chapter 4

I slept fitfully and wasn't very happy when Taylor woke me up the next morning by running the coffee grinder. The noise broke into a dream I'd been having that had something to do with Frank and nothing to do with reality. I stomped off to the shower, and my mood did not improve when the hot water gave out while I still had a head full of suds. By the time I'd toweled off, combed my hair and brushed my teeth, I was feeling a little more human but not very much more charitable toward Taylor for waking me up on my day off.

"You must've been thirsty last night," said Taylor with disgusting cheerfulness when I came out of the bedroom. "You're almost out of milk."

It's a good thing the last part of my shower had been cold. "Um, yeah, I guess I was."

She held up the two glasses I'd forgotten to wash. "Doing a little double-fisted drinking?"

"Frank Baker was here last night." Why should such an innocent statement make me feel so guilty?

Taylor raised an eyebrow. "And you served him milk? Caribou King, you can't seduce a man by plying him with milk."

"I wasn't trying to seduce him. Especially with you snoring away in my bed."

The playfulness fell away from her face and she frowned. "I don't snore."

"Of course you don't," I said, happy to have diverted her.

"So why was Frank here last night?"

"He wanted to make sure you were okay."

"Really? Wanted to make sure I was okay?" Taylor put emphasis on the word "I" and grinned at me.

"That's what I said. He stopped by on his way home."

"Stopped by on his way home?"

"Why are you repeating everything I say?"

"I thought Frank was living in your Dad's cabins."

"So?"

"Cara, the cabins are on the other side of town and a mile up the road to boot. Not too far from the mill, as I remember. You sure you want to stick to that story?"

I grabbed my sweater and started for the stairs. "I'm going to Mel's. If you're done making fun of me, you can come along."

Taylor laughed, and my anger melted. Her laughter was like the sound I imagined fairy bells making, and nobody can be angry with fairy bells in the air. She followed me down the steps. "When did you start locking the door? Did Frank say something to scare you?"

"I had to promise to lock up in order to get him to leave. Don't lock it behind us though. I don't have a key."

The fairy bells twinkled again. "You don't have a key to your own door?"

"I never lock my door. I'm sure it's around, but somebody woke me up too early this morning and pushed me out the door before I had a chance to look for it."

"I didn't push you out the door. You were running away so you wouldn't have to talk about Frank."

There was fog on the bay this morning, a sure sign that winter was coming. It dampened the usual noise, though on Thursdays there was never much noise to dampen. "There isn't anything to talk about. I told you he was just concerned. I bet Jack gave him an earful last night."

Taylor sighed and her face clouded like the fog. "I shouldn't have come back."

"Don't be ridiculous. You're always welcome, and I'm always happy to see you. Since you mentioned it though, I do wonder why you'd want to come back. There must be so many painful memories here."

Taylor didn't answer. Instead, she abruptly crossed the street and started down the boardwalk that edged the dock. I kept pace with her but said nothing, giving her time to collect her thoughts. At the end of the pier, she stopped and leaned on the rail, looking out at the fog. I listened to the muffled sound of the foghorn from the lighthouse and the gentle lap of the water against the pilings beneath us. "It was worse in Seattle. So much noise. Everybody going on with life as if nothing happened. I felt like I was betraying him." She stared out at the boats tied up in the marina. The sun was beginning to warm the air, pushing back the fog. "It hurts so much, Cara. People don't understand how it feels to wake up every morning and reach for him and not have him there."

"So you came back."

"I feel Johnny when I'm here. It's all I have left." She spun around and started walking again.

I hurried to catch up. "Why don't we go out to the house today? I have to crate yesterday's sales for Kenny, but after that I'm free."

"I thought you said it was rented."

"It is, but Mr. Peterson won't mind us stopping by, and I bet you'd feel better taking a look at the studio."

At the mention of the studio, Taylor slowed her pace and I was able to catch my breath. "Is it...?"

"Untouched. Just like Johnny left it. Dad put a lock on the door, but that's the only thing we've done."

A smile drifted across Taylor's face. "Do you know where that key is?"

"Dad has it. He knows how I am about keys."

"I always liked your dad."

"You go pick it up while I'm working, and by the time you get back, I'll be ready to head out."

"Thanks, Kenny. Have a safe trip." He honked his horn and waved an arm out the window as he pulled away from the gallery. Sales had been sluggish yesterday, so I'd had half the packages as I'd shipped the day before. Two cruise lines had paid their last visit of the season and would send their ships south for the winter so Coho Bay would close out the last week of the season working only three days instead of six. It had been a spectacular season for The Broken Antler, due in part to the demand for Johnny's work, but the interest in his paintings had spurred sales for other artists as well. I knew Johnny would have liked that.

When I finished, I went to Mel's to pick up the key to the boat. Taylor was waiting for me with a picnic basket, and we headed to the marina. She bubbled with conversation as we walked. Dad had been thrilled to see her. They'd hit it off from the time she'd stepped off the ferry from Juneau the summer she came to help me launch the gallery. She might look like a delicate flower, but she knew the business end of the hammer. She helped Dad with the finish carpentry in the apartment while Mom worked with me to lay out the exhibit space in the gallery.

We climbed into Dad's twenty-six-foot cabin cruiser, one of the smaller boats at the marina but larger than most of the pleasure craft I'd seen in Seattle. The water is a fixture of life here and while the Inside Passage is calm compared to the open ocean, in places the mountains can funnel the wind, stirring up the normally placid water. None of us would have felt comfortable running up to Juneau or over to Sitka in a smaller boat, and you needed a cabin to keep out the spray and the rain.

Taylor stowed the picnic basket while I fired up the motor. Or at least I tried to fire up the motor. It sputtered but didn't catch. I opened the hatch and grabbed a flashlight to take a look. There were many things I knew about, but engines were not one of them. I tinkered with it for a bit, then climbed up and hit the ignition again. Sputter. I tried again, then hollered to Taylor to hit the starter. Still nothing. I climbed back into the cabin.

"That's the extent of my knowledge of motors," I told her. "We'll have to get Dad."

"We can't. Your folks were headed out to the wilderness area when I left."

"Oh, shoot. I forgot about the moose count." I slapped the hatch lid shut. My mother was a wildlife biologist and my father an environmental scientist. Both worked for the State of Alaska, and every September they spent a week holed up in a forest service hut in a designated wilderness area documenting the moose population. I'd been so busy it had completely slipped my mind.

"You ladies need a little help?" We both turned and looked at Frank.

"The motor won't turn over, and I've run out of things to try."

"Sounds like the fuel filter. Got a spare?"

I opened the bin Dad used to store tools and spare parts and rummaged through the contents. "Doesn't look like it. Are you sure?"

"Let me take a look." Frank jumped down into the cruiser, and Taylor and I stepped aside to give him access to the hatch. He disappeared, and we could hear him muttering to himself. After about twenty minutes, his head reappeared. "Fire it up, Cara."

I hit the ignition. There was no sputtering this time, but there was no reassuring hum of the motor either. In fact, there was nothing at all. "You broke it."

"It was already broken."

"Well now, it's worse."

"Hang on." He disappeared, and I heard him muttering again. "Okay, try again."

"Still nothing," I called, though Frank could hear that as clearly as I could.

He climbed into the cabin and shut the hatch. "I just wanted to make sure. It's the fuel filter."

"Lovely. I've gotta catch Kenny so he can pick one up for me."

"He's already gone. You could try him on the radio, but he's probably out of range by now."

"He can't be. I just gave him my shipment."

"An hour and a half ago, Cara," said Taylor, looking at her watch.

"Cripes! I'm sorry, Tay. I'll talk to him tomorrow, and Dad can pop in the new filter when he gets back. Mr. Peterson will be leaving then, and we can get him moved out and you moved in all in one trip."

Frank studied Taylor, who'd been sitting silently on the bench outside the cabin while we worked on the motor. "You moving out to the island? Thought you were just here for a visit."

"Who told you that?" I asked when Taylor didn't respond.

"Simmons was telling Lennon. I was just along for the ride."

Taylor stood up and grabbed the picnic basket. "We'd better go, Cara. No point in sitting here all day."

"I could run you out there," Frank offered.

"Hey, that's an idea. Thanks," I said.

Taylor stood poised to climb out of the boat, her foot on the ladder, her back to Frank. "I wouldn't want to bother you."

"It's no bother."

I was puzzled by Taylor's reaction, but I decided to bail her out. "Tay's right. You're in your boat all week. Last thing you want to do on your day off is ferry people around the bay." Taylor turned to look at me. Her eyes, shiny with tears, tugged at my heart. She was proud, and the intense emotion of her first trip out to the island was best kept private.

Frank went along with me, though he had a puzzled look on his face. "You have a point there. Let me know when Kenny brings you that filter, and I'll put it in if you need to get out there before your dad gets back."

Taylor climbed out of the boat without another word and headed toward shore. I knew she would be in tears before she made it across the street.

"Sorry, just trying to help," said Frank, pulling my attention away from my retreating friend. I noticed his flannel shirt and old jeans were now smeared with grease.

"I appreciate your offer. So does Taylor. It's just that she hasn't been back to the house since Johnny died."

"And I would have been in the way."

"She wouldn't have wanted me there either, seeing his studio again for the first time. She just doesn't have a choice since she doesn't have a boat."

"How could she have lived on an island without a boat?"

"It was Johnny's. After he died, Jack took it back. Didn't bother anyone at the time because we all figured Taylor wouldn't be coming back."

Frank leaned against the wall of the cabin and crossed his arms. "She fell for Johnny pretty fast from what I hear."

"Did you ever meet Johnny?"

"Only in passing. He died not long after I moved here. I remember stocking up on bear spray."

"Lot of people did. Even locals get careless until someone gets hurt."

"Is that what happened to Johnny? He got careless?"

"I don't know. Taylor says she nagged him about going off on his hikes without some kind of protection, but he didn't listen. Johnny grew up here, so people thought he should have known better."

"Shouldn't he have?"

I turned away from him and looked out over the bay. "Johnny never thought about anything else when he was sketching. You could talk to him, and he wouldn't hear a word you said."

"And he went off that day to sketch?"

"Yes. He dropped Taylor at the gallery and headed out."

"Did she stay with you the rest of the day?"

"Yes. We were still together when we heard the news. Why so many questions?"

"Curious. She doesn't seem like his type."

"Why would you say that? You didn't even know Johnny, and you've barely met Taylor."

"I know her type." There was an odd flavor of bitterness in his words.

I rose to Taylor's defense. "And just what type is that?"

"The type who uses men. The type that's more interested in what's on the surface and doesn't care about what may be going on underneath."

His description was uncharitable, but as much as I wanted to, I couldn't deny its ring of truth. "She loved Johnny," I said at last, "whatever you may think."

"Didn't it surprise you? Her falling for him?"

I noticed Frank didn't ask if I'd been surprised that Johnny would fall for Taylor. I suppose that was a no-brainer. "Maybe. Johnny was sweet, but he was awkward and shy around outsiders. That's to be expected when you grow up in a town full of hermits."

"You're not a hermit."

"When you're asking people to spend thousands of dollars for something they can't even take back to the ship with them, you can't get away with hiding behind the cash register. Besides, people like to know the story behind the work, and I love telling those stories."

"So what was so special about Johnny?"

"To be honest, I think Tay fell in love with his art. Have you ever seen his paintings?" Frank shook his head. "He had a real gift. He used to tell me he just painted what he saw, but a camera can do that. Johnny captured the spirit of what he painted. You see it in his work. Place one of his paintings next to a less talented artist, and the difference is clear. They could be painting the same landscape, but in Johnny's you'd hear the waves and smell the pine. People come into the gallery and stand for hours looking at the only two paintings I have left. You can lose yourself in them."

"And Taylor lost herself?" It was clear by the look he was giving me that Frank did not believe me.

"Something like that." I pulled my sweater tight, hugging myself against the sudden chill, and I wasn't sure it was coming from the wind as much as the company.

Frank watched me, and I wondered if he even noticed the shift in mood. "Did Jack always hate her, or has it only been since his son died?"

I pulled the key out of the ignition and pushed him out of the cabin. "Enough of your questions."

"I feel like I came in during the middle of this movie. I like to know what I missed." We climbed out of the boat and walked toward the stairs that led up to the boardwalk.

"Except it's not a movie. These are real people with real pain. Tay's had more loss in her life than anyone deserves. It's not fair what happened to Johnny."

"Especially for Johnny."

I stopped walking and looked intently at Frank, wondering if he was making another joke, but there wasn't a trace of humor in his expression. I lowered my eyes. "Especially for Johnny."

There was no sign of Taylor when I got back to my apartment. I dropped my sweater on the couch, picked up the book I'd been reading the night before, and settled into the chair next to the window. I thumbed through until I found my place and started to read. As anyone could tell by looking at my bookcases, I love to read. I mean, I *love* it. When I open the pages of a book, the world around me disappears. I'd told Frank that Johnny couldn't hear me when he was at his easel. Well, I couldn't hear anything when I was lost in the pages of a good book. I can read through anything, even an Alaskan blizzard, which my father calls hurricanes of the north. I stock up on books in the fall, and then all winter long, tucked away in my cabin, the world opens up to me in their pages.

I only live in town during cruise ship season. Come October, I pack up and head for a sturdy and snug log cabin, deep in the woods, a few hundred feet from the cabin where my parents live. Some people might not want to live so close to their parents, but they are good about giving me my privacy, and, in turn, I'm good about respecting theirs. There is a third cabin for Mel and Bent, but people got used to eating at the restaurant during the first season and clamored for them to keep it open during the winter. Families who ate there contributed food since Bent didn't have time to hunt or grow a garden, and unlike the season when the Health Department was prone to make unannounced inspections, nobody said a word when he served home-butchered meat and home-canned fruit and vegetables.

Since their first winter in town, Mel and Bent had been after me to stick around, and I was giving it serious consideration. Mom and Dad had stubbornly resisted moving, and I couldn't blame them. They didn't have a place in town, so they'd have to live in Mel's guest room and that might be a little too much togetherness even for my family. I didn't like the idea of them being out in the woods by themselves all winter though, so if they didn't come to town, I doubted I would. I'd have to make up my mind soon. Next week the ships would sail away for the last time, and most of the population of Coho Bay would scatter until spring.

The door banged open, then slammed shut. "Cara!"

Jumping up, I leaned over the banister and looked down at Taylor. She was fumbling with the locks. "What's the matter?" I called down to her.

"Call the police!"

"He's out fishing. What's wrong?"

"What do you mean, he's out fishing?"

"It's Thursday."

"So the whole police force is out fishing?"

"Dan is the whole police force. What's wrong?"

"What is wrong with this town?" She punctuated every word with a stomp on the next step as she climbed up to me. "We could all be murdered in our beds, and they'd say, *sorry, it's Thursday.*"

"Nobody gets murdered in Coho Bay."

Taylor threw open the refrigerator door. "Milk! Why don't you have anything to drink in this place? What's the matter with you?"

"Why do you need the police?" I could see she was upset, but her hysterical attack on me and my town was beginning to grate on me.

"What I need is a beer. Surely there must be one beer somewhere in this town?"

"Not on Thursday. Tay, focus! Why do you need the police?"

She let out a string of profanity. One or two of the words she unleashed I'd never heard before, but I didn't think now was the time to congratulate her for creative swearing. Instead, I went into the living room and sank back into my reading chair. "When you're done being a drama queen, you can tell me what's wrong."

She let out what I can only describe as a primal yell. I really have to tip my hat to Tay. She does drama better than anyone I know. She clenched her hands into fists and took a deep breath. "Somebody is trying to kill me."

She had my attention now. "What? When?"

"Just now."

"Somebody tried to kill you, and you're giving me crap about milk?"

"Do you want to hear this or not?"

I sat back again. "You almost had me there. Do you want to try again, this time without the cheesy music?"

Taylor came into the living room and perched on the arm of the couch. "You're not making this easier."

"I'm sorry. Go on with your story."

"I went for a walk."

"After you left me at the boat?"

"That jerk."

"Who?"

"You're defending him? Because you finally noticed he's got six-pack abs, suddenly he can do no wrong?"

"Frank? When did you see his abs?"

"Can we not make this about Frank?"

"I'm not making it about Frank. You're the one who brought him up. Why is he a jerk all of a sudden?"

She put her hands on her temples and started massaging. "You are not taking this seriously."

"It helps that no one's trying to kill me." She looked like she was going to throw something at me. "Fine. I'm taking it seriously. Tell me your story."

"I went for a walk to clear my head."

"Carrying a picnic basket?"

"What?"

"You left with the picnic basket, though come to think of it, you didn't come home with it."

"Why are you obsessing about the picnic basket?"

"I'm hungry."

"Oh. My. God." Taylor got up and stomped to the kitchen. She threw open the pantry cupboard and grabbed a box of saltines. Slamming the cupboard shut, she stomped back to the living room and thrust it at me. "Here!"

I took the box. "Gee, thanks. Now, go on. Where'd you go?"

"Out past the cannery." The cannery processed the salmon that gave Coho Bay its name. It was about a half mile past Mel's, down a dirt road that ran along that side of the bay. There was a marina where the fishing boats moored, and in the summer a cloud of gulls feasted on what my mother called salmon waste products. I called them gut piles, but hey, she was the biologist. This time of year the fishermen consolidated into a few large boats and left to go crabbing in Bristol Bay. It was a horribly dangerous job and more than a few men had been seriously injured or killed over the years, but crabbing was big money, so the boats kept running.

"Someone tried to kill you at the cannery?"

"Yes! Well, no. Not at the cannery. I'm not sure when he started following me. I didn't notice him until I was almost back to town."

"Someone didn't try to kill you. Someone followed you."

Taylor turned on me, defiance in her every feature. "Well, he could have killed me if I hadn't run!"

"Okay, I believe you." I popped a cracker into my mouth. "Who was it? Oooh, was it Jack?"

"I'm glad you're enjoying yourself." She sat down on the arm of the couch. "I don't know. He was wearing a black raincoat with the hood pulled down."

"On a clear day?"

"That's what I said! Why are you asking so many questions? When I got to Mel's, the door was locked. I know, it's Thursday. Anyway, I knocked but she didn't answer, and I couldn't wait, so I ran home as fast as I could."

I went to the window and looked up the street. "Whoever he was, he's gone now. What makes you think he was following you?"

"He wasn't exactly out for a stroll."

"He might have been."

"Cara!"

I raised my hands in surrender. "Okay, he was following you. What makes you think he was trying to kill you?"

"Why else would he be following me?"

I opened my mouth to answer, but she glared at me, so I kept my thoughts to myself. Her energy spent, Taylor slid off the arm and lay on the couch, staring up at the ceiling. "I thought it would be easier here."

"Time heals all things, Tay."

"That's crap," she countered, but her voice was more sad than angry. "They told me that when I lost my family. People have no idea what to say to that kind of loss, so they fall back on that old line." She looked up at me. "It was crap then, and it's crap now."

Chapter 5

"I didn't hear Taylor knock yesterday. You say she was pounding at the door?" Mel was elbow-deep in bread dough, her hair tied back and her apron white with flour. Spicy, hot cabbage burgers were always on the menu the last week of the season and were a favorite of both cruisers and locals. Bent was frying donuts, something he'd gotten up early to do since I'd burned too many batches to be trusted with the job. I was washing pots as usual.

"That's what she said. I don't know how you could've missed her." Bent and Mel exchanged glances, and Mel's face reddened. "Moving right along, do you think it was Jack? Frank said he was ranting about Tay all the way home."

"When did you start hanging out with Frank?" asked Mel.

"He stopped by the boat when Tay and I were trying to head out to the island yesterday. That reminds me, I have to ask Kenny to pick up a fuel filter. I couldn't get it started, and Frank said he thought that was the problem."

"Not again," sighed Bent, fishing donuts out of the oil and laying them on a drainer. He put another batch in the oil, then sprinkled powdered sugar over the cooling ones. He'd move them to a serving dish before fishing out that batch, repeating the process until he'd made enough for the breakfast rush.

I leaned against the sink, watching him. "What do you mean?"

"Your dad and I just put a new fuel filter on the boat three weeks ago. If it's bad already, we'll have to tear apart the motor to find out what's going on when he gets back."

"You'd better hold off, Cara," said Mel. "You don't want to be stuck in the middle of the bay if the motor goes out."

"I have to go get Mr. Peterson on Thursday. He's only got the house through the end of the season."

"Call him. I bet he'd be happy to stay on a few extra days."

"I suppose."

"If he has connections to make, I'm sure someone could run you out there." Mel covered the huge bowl of dough with a clean dish towel and set it in a corner to rise. She gathered up her dirty dishes and dumped them in the sink for me, then cleaned the worktable and started putting together meat and egg casseroles.

"Like Frank," said Bent.

"Which brings me back to the subject."

"What subject?" asked Mel.

"The guy who was chasing Tay."

"Just because she was running, doesn't mean anyone was chasing her." Mel filled three large baking dishes and, after sprinkling a few handfuls of cheese on the top, slid them into the oven. More dishes hit the sink, but at least she was ready now to turn her attention to the family breakfast. The smell of the donuts was making me hungry.

"She wouldn't lie to me."

"I'm not saying she lied. I'm saying she might be jumpy after that run-in with Jack. She might have read something into it that wasn't there. Poor guy might've been out for a walk."

"Wearing a raincoat?" I asked.

Mel shrugged. "Outsiders are always cold. Maybe it was the only coat he had."

"Why didn't she call Dan if she was so scared?" asked Bent, sugaring the last batch of donuts.

"On a Thursday?" Mel and I said in two-part harmony.

"He's not dead on Thursdays. He's just off duty."

"Do you remember the last time somebody bothered him on a Thursday when it wasn't an emergency?" I asked.

"You've got a point there," agreed Bent as he headed out to the dining room.

Mel set a plate of blueberry pancakes on the worktable and handed me a fork. "Leave the dishes. You'll be late."

"What do you know about Frank?" I asked, pulling off my apron and perching on a stool across from her, watching her make more pancakes.

"As much as you do."

"But you see him every day."

"So do you, and I'm not the one whose been flirting with him."

"Am I the only one who didn't know he was flirting with me?"

"How could you not know? You were flirting too."

I threw up my hands. "See? And I didn't know that either. Obviously I'm not doing it right."

"You're doing it fine."

"Do you think he thinks I've been flirting?"

"Want me to pass him a note when I see him in class? C'mon, Cara."

"When did he get to be so good-looking?"

"How good-looking do you think he is?"

"I don't know. Romance-novel cover?"

Mel laughed. "You've got it bad. Frank's cute, but he's not that cute."

I could still hear Bent moving chairs in the dining room. I lowered my voice and leaned across the worktable. "He showed up at my apartment in the middle of the night."

"Last night?" Mel put down her fork and stared openmouthed at me.

"No, the night before. After he and Dan took Jack home."

"And you're just now getting around to telling me this?"

"I forgot."

Mel picked up her fork again. "You forgot about a 'romance-novel cover' gorgeous man dropping by your apartment in the middle of the night? I'm sure that happens all the time."

"Do you want to hear this or make fun of me?"

"I can do both. What did he want?"

"He wanted me to lock my door and keep my gun loaded."

"Because of Jack?"

"Yep. Then he said he saw someone standing outside city hall, watching the apartment."

She dropped her fork this time. "Did you see him?"

"I saw someone's feet, but it was dark and the guy was standing under the awning. Frank went out to tell him to give it up and go to bed. I saw the two of them, or at least their feet standing together, so whoever it was couldn't have been too scary."

"But it puts another light on Taylor's story. Maybe you should keep your gun handy. At least until the season's over."

"I suppose you're right. At least I'm safe in the gallery." The town had installed a system of silent alarms in each store since merchants handled a significant amount of cash.

"You should tell Dan about it. The guy's probably seasonal."

"You say that when anything bad happens."

"And I'm usually right. If it was a local, he'd know the whole town would come after him. Seasonals think they can get away with anything and be gone before anybody figures it out."

I finished my pancakes, slid off the stool, and headed for the back door. "The gallery calls. What's for dinner tonight?"

"Whatever I decide to make for you," said Bent, coming back into the kitchen.

I pulled on my hooded rain jacket and went out into the predawn rain. It was just a drizzle, but it was icy cold, a sure sign that the moose would be heading into lower country, passing near the forest service cabin where my parents were poised to count them. Of course, it wasn't only moose that migrated, but because they were the largest animals in the woods, the health of the moose population gave a good indication of the health of the forest.

I pulled the hood down over my face and lowered my head, pushing through the wall of moisture as quickly as my feet would carry me. I wanted to get to the gallery before I was completely drenched, or it would be hours before I would feel warm again. Accustomed to having the boardwalk to myself at that hour, I didn't see the person in front of me until I slammed into him, sending us both to the ground. I sat up sputtering. "I'm sorry. I didn't see you."

His back was to me, and all I could see was a black raincoat with a hood pulled up. My heart skipped a beat until he spoke. "You must've been a linebacker in college."

"Frank! I'm so sorry."

"You said that." He stood up and offered me his arm. "You should seriously think about football if the whole art gallery thing doesn't work out."

"I actually did play football, but only in high school. We didn't have enough boys to field a team, so I got drafted."

"Somehow that doesn't surprise me."

"I wasn't a linebacker though. I was a quarterback. It was one of the only times it came in handy to be so tall."

"I like tall women."

In spite of the cold, I felt my face turn hot. "Let's not stand out here in the rain." We crossed the street and hurried to the gallery door. "What are you doing up and about this early?"

"Checking on you. Making sure you're okay."

"At five thirty in the morning?" I unlocked the gallery and held the door open for him. We shed our raincoats and hung them on a rack in the entry to keep them from dripping all over the gallery's waxed wood floors.

"What were you doing wandering around in the rain?" he asked, ignoring my question.

"I need coffee," I said. If he was going to ignore my question, I was going to ignore his, at least until I had started a fresh pot. "I help Mel and Bent get ready for the breakfast rush every morning. They feed me, then I come here to get my shipment ready for Kenny. Now can I ask you something?"

"You don't have a shipment this morning. Gallery was closed yesterday."

"I have other paperwork I do on Fridays. My question?"

"Shoot."

"Why are you suddenly so nosy?"

"I've always been nosy."

"You've never had more than ten words to say to me before."

"I've always had more than ten words. You just never let me say them."

There was a shift in the conversation that had nothing to do with our actual words. I busied myself by pouring coffee until I could trust my voice. I held a cup up for Frank, but he shook his head. "In my defense, you've always struck me as a bit..."

He moved close and put his hands on either side of me, resting on the counter. He leaned his head in and whispered, "Dashing?"

His nearness was making it hard for me to concentrate, but I managed to stand my ground. "Obnoxious."

He put his hands over his heart. "Ouch."

I slipped away from him and crossed to my desk. "So who did Mr. Shoes turn out to be?"

"Mr. Shoes?"

"The guy you thought was watching my apartment."

"I don't know."

"He wouldn't tell you?"

"I didn't see him. He was gone by the time I got there."

I took a long, slow drink from my cup. Why was he lying? I decided against confronting him about it and instead changed the subject. "Bent says he and Dad put a new fuel filter on the boat a few weeks ago."

Was that a twitch at the corner of his mouth? Had he been lying about that too, or was Taylor's paranoia wearing off on me? "That doesn't sound good. Your Dad should overhaul that motor before you try to take the boat out. Tell him to give me a yell if he needs help."

I relaxed a bit. "Bent said the same thing. I'm hoping it's something quick and simple. He's not back until

Wednesday night, and I really need to get out to the
island on Thursday." I hoped the boat wouldn't need
any parts because there were none to be had in town.
Dad would have to ride into Juneau with Kenny if he
needed anything, and that would cost him most of the
day. Nothing happens in a hurry here.

"Your friend that desperate?"

I shook my head. "Tay could wait, but I have a
renter I need to pick up."

"My offer stands. I'd be happy to run you out there."

"I might take you up on that if Bent and Dad can't
get the boat running in time."

"Which reminds me, I've been meaning to talk to
you about moving back to the apartment for the winter.
When are you moving out?"

"I don't know. Mel has been after me to stay in town
this winter, but I don't want to leave Mom and Dad in
the woods by themselves."

"They lived out there when the two of you were just
kids, didn't they?"

"Not in the winter. We wouldn't have been able to
go to school from out there, so they built a house in
town."

"Why don't they live there now?"

"Because they converted it to a restaurant when Mel
and Bent got married."

"Ah, I see the light. Well, if you decide to stay in
town, I guess I could go live in your cabin and keep
your folks company."

"Hey, that's an idea. Let me think on it."

"So where are these paintings of Lennon's?"

"Snow. Jonathan Snow is the name he painted
under."

"I don't blame him. Why would anyone name your
kid John when your last name is Lennon?"

"It's his father's name, only his dad has gone by Jack for as long as I can remember."

"I didn't know that. Makes some sense now."

"Come on, I'll show you the two I have left."

We walked through the darkened gallery to where the paintings were hung. Positioning Frank for maximum impact, I switched on the lights that highlighted the canvases. I watched his face, but there was no reaction. Feeling a little disappointed, I bit my lip to keep from talking about Johnny's deft use of color and texture to create areas of light and shadow, closeness and depth. I didn't point out his perfect sense of proportion, or that what he chose to include and what he opted to leave out took a living landscape and recast it in the artist's vision, creating an emotional impact that left one breathless. There was so much I could have said about the enchantment of Johnny's paintings, but I chose to say none of them. You couldn't give someone an appreciation of a work of art with words. They either felt it, or they didn't.

Frank stepped forward and looked intently at the paintings. After a few minutes he stepped back and looked down at me. "These are the only ones you have left?"

"I'm afraid so. Johnny had been dabbling for years, but he hadn't been painting full time for more than a couple of years when he died. There just wasn't time..." I turned away.

Frank put his hands on my shoulders. His touch was gentle, soothing. "You miss him."

"Of course I do." I swiped at the tear with my fingers, grateful for once that I'm allergic to mascara so I never wear it. At least Frank wouldn't see me with tear tracks.

He gave my shoulders a squeeze, then dropped his hands and moved toward the door, weaving his way unerringly through the sculptures in the dim light that signaled dawn. I followed slowly, gathering myself as I went, so by the time we reached the entryway I was composed. Frank looked at me for a long moment. "You don't like me," he said, pulling on his coat.

He'd caught me off guard. "No. I wouldn't say that. Why do you think so?"

He reached out and ran his fingertips across my cheek. The touch was so unexpected I flinched as though he'd burned me. The corner of his mouth turned up. "No reason."

"Town full of hermits, remember?" I was shaking. Taylor would have said something cute and sexy, and Frank would have melted into her arms. What was wrong with me?

"Do you make everything into a joke?" He tipped my chin up so I couldn't help but look at him. Through sheer force of will, I managed to hold myself still. His eyes were the most amazing gray, tinged just a bit with blue. A girl could lose herself in a pair of eyes like that. I forced myself to look away, and he went out into the street, turning toward the marina. The drizzle had become a torrent, and I wondered if the cruise ship, the lights of which were barely visible, would cancel its excursions. If they did, maybe he would be back. The thought brought I smile to my face, then I frowned, remembering his lie about Mr. Shoes. Frank Baker might be wicked sexy, but he was hiding something from me and it would be safer if I kept him at a distance until I found out what it was.

Fridays were always busy at The Broken Antler, even when it wasn't raining as it had been all day long. Friday had been my best sales day ever since the second season, when this particular line started calling at Coho Bay. I don't know what was different about that cruise line, but their passengers came on shore ready, even eager, to buy. They were a shopkeeper's dream and 'Thank God, it's Friday' had taken on new meaning for me. Taylor joined me in the gallery shortly before the first tender docked, and we'd been run off our feet all day. We didn't even have time to slip down to Mel's to grab lunch. Instead, we raided the supply of energy bars I kept in the backroom for days like this. When the ship's whistle blew at four, beckoning cruisers to the last tender, the gallery finally emptied. Locking the door behind the last customer, I slumped against it.

"It's been a day, hasn't it?" Taylor asked. Her face bore a reflection of my own exhaustion, though without my underlying happiness at knowing I'd earned both my artists and me a good amount of money this day.

"I can't believe how many pieces we sold. I'll have to crunch the numbers, but it might just be the best day we've ever had. Kenny's gonna have a full boat tomorrow, that's for sure."

Taylor pulled the cash drawer open and started counting money, checking the amounts against the register report. "Sheesh!" she said, filling out a deposit slip and tucking the money into a bank bag. "I had no idea the gallery had become so successful."

I joined her at the counter, and she handed me the report. "Fridays are always good, but we really have done well this year. You should know that, considering the size of the deposits I've made to Johnny's account this summer."

Taylor handed me the bag. "I can't touch Johnny's money. I don't even get a statement."

"The estate hasn't settled yet? What's the holdup?"

Taylor didn't answer. She walked over to stand in front of Johnny's paintings. "I wish he could know he could have made a living with his art."

"Was there any doubt?"

"Jack thought Johnny ought to be making something substantial, like furniture, instead of painting nice little pictures for old women. He painted as much as he could over the winters, but Jack made sure he was too busy and too tired in the summer. When Johnny quit working so he could concentrate on his painting, Jack went ballistic."

"What'd he say? No, wait. It's none of my business."

"He threw Johnny out of the house. Of course, Johnny didn't care, because he had the island. His mother left him the property free and clear when she died, but he'd just rented it out."

"I remember you two fixing it up after you got married, but I never knew Johnny moved out there because he and Jack had been fighting. I always thought they were close." I sighed. "I feel responsible since I was the one who pestered him to let me exhibit his paintings."

Taylor looked at me, her eyes misty. "You were the first person to believe in him. That meant everything."

"You're the one who made it possible for him to follow his dream. I just gave him a way to have his work seen."

Taylor walked up to one of the paintings and ran her fingers along the frame. "Would it be so horrible if you didn't sell this one?"

The painting depicted the view from the island, looking toward town. It captured his love for his birthplace while celebrating the natural beauty that drew tourists to Coho Bay. I thought it was the best painting he'd done, completed only weeks before he died. If I were Taylor, I'd want to keep it too. "It wouldn't be horrible at all."

"I feel him here." Tears streamed down her cheeks as she leaned her head against the frame.

I stood awkwardly, not knowing whether I should comfort her or if that would be an intrusion. I'd only seen Taylor cry that one time on the pier right after Johnny died. She'd kept an iron grip on her emotions afterward, and it had raised a few eyebrows around town. She hadn't wanted to go back to the house, so I'd given her the use of my apartment and had gone to stay in Mel's guest room. If she'd cried alone at night, I didn't know. She had left town before snow flew.

As those memories played in my head, Taylor took a tissue from her pocket and wiped her eyes. "Sorry to dump on you like this."

"We'll get it moved to the house as soon as you're settled."

There was a knock at the door, and I went to open it. Dan stepped into the entry, dripping wet. "I don't have to ask if it's still raining," I greeted him. "Can I take your coat?"

"Not gonna stay that long. I just wanted to ask you and Ms. Lennon about those men you saw."

"How did you hear about them?" I asked as Taylor joined us at the door. Dad and I had built the entry big enough to accommodate ten people taking off coats and hanging up wet umbrellas. Gallery owners we'd spoken to in other port cities had warned us that there needed to be plenty of space because people weren't always willing to wait. It was odd that with just the three of us, the entry was feeling cramped.

Dan was slow to answer. "Mel told me."

"There was only one man." Taylor's voice sounded surprisingly crisp, considering her tears only moments ago. "In a black raincoat with his hood pulled low."

"Frank has a black hooded raincoat. I noticed it today," I said, feeling a twinge of guilt as though I were ratting him out.

"You don't think it could have been Frank?" asked Taylor, eyes wide.

"What about your guy, Cara?" Dan asked, looking at me and ignoring her.

"You have a guy?" asked Taylor.

"It was nothing," I assured her. "I didn't want you to worry."

"Is that why you started locking the door?"

"You're locking your door?" asked Dan. "I thought you said it was nothing."

I held up my hands, feeling like a Ping-Pong ball trapped between them. "Ask Frank. He saw the guy from my apartment, and then he went down to talk to him, though this morning he claimed the guy was gone when he got there."

"Frank was in the apartment?" asked Taylor. "When was this?"

"The night Jack went off on you at Mel's. Look, Dan, I didn't see anything but the guy's feet, standing over there." I nodded toward city hall.

"So did Frank talk to him or didn't he?" asked Dan.

"That's the weird part."

"*That's* the weird part?" asked Taylor, but I ignored her.

"After he left, I looked out and saw that one set of feet had been joined by a second. Of course, I assumed it was Frank, but he says not."

"When did you talk to Frank?" asked Taylor.

"I ran into him this morning on the way back from Mel's," I told Taylor. I massaged the back of my neck, which had grown sore as the conversation went on.

Dan stepped out the door, letting in the sound and scent of the rain. "I'll check it out. You ladies call me if you see either of them again."

"Even on Thursday?" asked Taylor.

"Don't be a wise guy," he told her and disappeared into the storm.

I shrugged into my raincoat and went back to the counter to get the deposit bag. "Let's go see what Bent made for dinner."

Taylor picked up one of the bright yellow umbrellas stamped with the Coho Bay Merchant Association logo that I kept by the door. I found them garish, but only a few of them seemed to disappear every year, so the color served its purpose. We dropped off the deposit at the bank and splashed across the street to Mel's. Despite our raincoats and the ugly umbrella, we were soaked to the skin by the time we made it to our barstools.

"Most people go around the puddles instead of through them," said Mel, shaking her head at us. She poured me a cup of coffee and put hot water and a selection of tea bags in front of Taylor.

"Most people don't have any fun," I retorted. Taylor giggled, and I cradled my cup in my hands until feeling returned to my half-frozen fingers.

"Snowing yet?" Mel asked.

"It feels cold enough, but it's still rain."

"I hope the snow holds off till next week."

"I don't know. Snow didn't hurt sales last season."

"For you, maybe. I was stuck with a diner full of people nursing coffee and staring out the window."

"What's for dinner?" Taylor asked, breaking into the banter. She knew Mel and I could go on for hours if not interrupted. "It smells amazing."

"End of season stew," answered Mel as she headed into the kitchen.

"What in the heck is 'end of season stew,' or is it one of those things that's better if I don't ask?"

I jumped at the sound of Frank's voice close to my elbow. "Where'd you come from?" One side of his mouth turned up in a half smile that sent my pulse racing. *Liar, liar, liar,* I chanted to myself to counter the physical reaction his nearness was setting off in me. *Keep your distance, Cara.* Oh, but he smelled good, with the scents of the bay and the rain mixed up with something indefinably masculine. I shook my head to break the spell.

"St. Paul, originally. Tonight I'm running late. Had to hose out the boat."

Neither Taylor nor I wanted to hear the rest of that story. Sometimes hapless cruisers assumed their ability to manage the calm water of the Inner Passage, while riding on a ship the size of an aircraft carrier meant they would have sea legs in a cabin cruiser on a choppy bay. I felt bad for them, but the result made me glad I worked in a gallery instead of on a boat. I decided to ignore his excuse and answer his question. "End of season stew is what you'd think it would be. Bent clearing out leftovers."

"Sounds… appetizing."

"It tastes better than it sounds."

"Has he thought about end-of-season pizza instead? I eat just about anything if you put it on pizza."

"As a matter of fact, that does sound good." We looked up to find Mel standing in front of us with two bowls of stew. "I'll mention it to Bent."

"Tell him I'll taste-test for him."

"I'll do that. I think he has some cabbage burgers left if you don't want stew."

"Why don't you just bring me whatever you want to get rid of?" This inspired a peal of laughter from Taylor, who knew from experience not to give Bent so large an opening. He looked from her to me. "What am I missing?"

"Nothing," I said, kicking Taylor under the counter. "Bring him the stew, Mel."

"You take all my fun away," said Taylor with a mock pout.

"To go?" asked Mel. When Frank gave her a puzzled frown, she added, "You're just standing there. Wait, you're not into that new stand-up-to-eat craze are you?" She turned to me. "Would you believe I had a couple ask me where the standing area was? They said it's all the rage. You actually choose to stand up while you eat, can you imagine? Like a horse! Why would people do that?"

Shaking her head at the oddities of people who lived anywhere other than Coho Bay, Mel left to get bread for us and stew for Frank. When she returned, she placed the bread between Taylor and me and looked at Frank. "You aren't really gonna stand, are you?"

"I'll give it a go," he said, winking at me. Mel put his stew bowl down and grabbed a set of silverware from a bin behind the counter.

"Don't mind me if I run over you." She brushed past him to get into the dining room to bus a table. Before she could finish cleaning it, three men sat down. She greeted them warmly and pushed past Frank again to get to the kitchen with their order.

"Scoot over, Tay," I said. "If we don't want Mel channeling her inner linebacker, we'd better make room for Frank."

Taylor gave me a look, then got off her stool, moved it over as far as it would go, and climbed back up. I followed suit, and Frank was mostly out of Mel's way when she sailed out of the kitchen with a tray of food. She dropped bread and a bowl of stew in front of him as she passed.

"Busy tonight," said Frank, watching her go.

It was disappointing to have the old, dreary Frank back. I kind of liked the superhero, but if he was going to lie to me, it was probably safer that he went back to being boring. "Did Dan talk to you?"

"What about?"

"Mr. Shoes."

"Oh. Yeah. Not much to say."

"Only what the guy told you when you talked to him."

Frank's spoon faltered. "I told you this morning I never talked to him."

"That's what you said."

He put down his spoon. "Meaning?"

"Meaning I saw you."

"You saw me. Talking to a pair of shoes."

"You know what I mean. You left to confront him, and I saw two sets of shoes under the awning."

"Table opened up, Frank," Mel said as she traded our empty stew bowls for ones full of vanilla ice cream. She nodded toward the window. "Why don't you sit down, and I'll bring your dessert out in a minute?"

Frank opened his mouth but must have thought better of it. "Ladies," he said, nodding to us. He picked up his napkin and silverware and headed over to the vacant table.

"I don't get it," I said to Taylor, keeping my voice low. "Why does he keep lying?"

"Maybe he doesn't want to scare you."

"Why would I be scared?"

Taylor looked over my shoulder. "He's watching us."

I resisted the urge to look. "I don't care."

She stopped looking at Frank and popped a spoonful of ice cream into her mouth. "You don't have a lot to choose from up here though."

"He lied to me."

Taylor ate another spoonful, her face thoughtful. "I wonder what he really told dapper Dan."

I think I may have snorted ice cream through my nose. Not pleasant. "Don't call him that. Somebody's gonna hear you."

"They call him worse things behind his back."

"I've never heard anybody call him names."

Taylor looked at me, her expression a touch condescending. I'd seen that look on her face before, the first time I met her. I'd gone to a party, and my date had abandoned me for another girl. She'd asked me what was wrong, and when I'd told her, she'd given me this look that was slightly superior, slightly amused and something else that I couldn't quite put my finger on. From that day to this, I hadn't seen that look directed at me again, and I didn't like seeing it now.

"Nobody's going to call him anything in front of you, Cara. I bet you don't hear half the crap they say about me."

Now, there she was wrong. I'd heard what people said about Taylor when she married Johnny, and far uglier, what they'd said after he died and she left Coho Bay. If people were talking about Dan, I would have heard it. I didn't want to hurt her feelings, so instead of arguing the point, I changed the subject. "What did Dan want to talk to you about the other day?"

Her eyes became shielded. "Are you ready to go or are you going to stay and help Mel?"

Without waiting for an answer, she jumped off her stool and headed for the door. I watched, trying to force my mouth closed as she stopped at the entry only long enough to put on her raincoat and pick up a yellow umbrella. Without looking back, she was gone. Movement by the window attracted my attention. Frank was up and heading for the door. He didn't appear to be in any hurry, but he didn't as much as turn his head on his way out. He grabbed his raincoat and pushed out the door only a few steps behind Taylor.

Mel came up beside me. "What's up with that?"

"I have no idea." I grabbed a gray tub and a wet cloth from behind the counter and went out into the dining room, piling dishes into the tub and washing off tables as they emptied.

It was almost closing time when it struck me that Taylor didn't have a key to the apartment. I'd found mine, but I hadn't made one for her because I knew she would be leaving soon and we were always together. Why hadn't she come back when she'd realized she was locked out? Taylor could be stubborn and proud, but standing in the pouring rain in the dark, especially when she'd been so scared only the night before would have been too much even for her. Maybe she hadn't locked the door when she'd left the apartment to come to the gallery. Of course that must be it.

I walked back to the kitchen, still thinking about Taylor and wondering why Frank had followed her. He hadn't come back either. Bent and Mel broke apart when I entered, both of their faces turning red. "Don't be embarrassed, you guys. Married people are allowed to kiss. I have to go check on Tay." I dropped my soiled apron in the hamper.

"What's the matter with Taylor?" asked Bent. His voice sounded normal, and most of the red had faded from his cheeks.

"She took off in a huff after dinner and hasn't been back."

"Why would she come back?" asked Mel.

"She doesn't have a key."

"Since when do you lock your door?" asked Bent.

"Since two days ago. Sheesh, where have you been?" I headed through the dining room to pick up my raincoat. I was glad I'd worn the lined one, but it wouldn't be long before I'd have to trade my raincoat for my winter jacket. It felt colder than the thermometer at the bank read, what with the humidity and the wind coming off the bay. I wished I'd thought to put my gloves in my pockets.

I walked fast, keeping an eye out for strange men in black raincoats this time, but the street was empty. I reached my door and wasn't sure whether to be relieved or worried when I found it locked. I fumbled with the key, my hands too cold at first to work the lock. When I finally got it open, I flipped the light switch, grateful for what little warmth sunk down to the entry from the pellet stove above. Even so, the entry felt like a sauna compared to outside.

"Taylor?" The echo may have been my imagination, but it wasn't my imagination that no one answered. I ran up the steps and searched the apartment. Two minutes later I was headed back to Mel's. She stopped pouring coffee and stared at me. I hurried past her into the kitchen.

Mel handed the pot to her customer and followed me. "I take it she's not there," she said as soon as we hit the kitchen.

I shook my head. "Maybe she went somewhere with Frank."

"Why Frank?" asked Bent.

We ignored him. "Was it locked when you got there?" asked Mel, and I nodded. "Why wouldn't she just come get the key?"

"I don't know, but she's not at the apartment. Where else could she have gone?"

"Why would she be with Frank?" We still didn't answer Bent's question.

"Do you have a cell phone number for him?" I asked, but Mel shook her head. "Maybe I should call Dan."

"Why Dan? Did Frank kidnap her?"

I went to the phone while Mel stared at Bent. "Why would Frank kidnap Taylor?"

"That's what I'm asking you."

"Nobody kidnapped anybody," I said, picking up the receiver.

Mel brought Bent up to speed while I counted the rings on Dan's phone. Who sets their phone to ring seven times before it goes to voice mail? I left a message and turned to look at my sister, who was starting to put away food for the night.

"You think he's asleep?" I looked up at the clock. It was high time I was sleeping. I didn't know how Mel and Bent managed to survive on six hours of sleep every day all season long. I'd be dragging at the gallery tomorrow if I didn't get to bed soon.

"Who, Dan? Maybe."

"What time was he in tonight?"

"He wasn't. I haven't seen him since lunch, and he was late for that. Sounded like he was coming down with something. Maybe he went home early."

"He stopped by the gallery as I was closing."

"What was he doing there?" We heard the front door open, and Bent went to see if the last customer had left.

"Asking about Mr. Shoes and the guy who followed Tay home. He said you told him about them."

"I asked what he was gonna do about it. Obviously you hadn't told him, so I did."

Bent returned with Dan behind him. "Nobody's home at Frank's," Bent reported. "Coffee, Dan?"

"Hoping not to be awake that long." Dan looked at me. "You sure she's not at your place? In the gallery maybe?"

"Tay doesn't have a key to the gallery either."

"Well, I'll check Frank's boat, but if it's rockin,' I ain't knockin.'" He was the only one who laughed.

"Tay barely knows Frank."

"Don't just stand there making stupid jokes. Go. Find them." Mel's voice had the high-pitched quality it got when she was nervous or scared.

"It's okay, baby," said Bent, squeezing her hands until she nodded. "C'mon, Dan, we'll check Frank's boat, but if they aren't there, I for one am going to bed."

"Bentley Milford Andrews!" Mel only dragged Bent's full name out on special occasions and none of them good. Even when they got married, Bent made sure the minister used his nickname. Given his full name, I hadn't blamed him. "They may be out there hurt somewhere, and you stand here laughing!" She started to cry.

Bent put his arms around her and whispered something I couldn't hear. Mel's shoulders visibly relaxed, and the tears stopped. He gave her a kiss that was a little bit longer than it needed to be while Dan shifted his feet back and forth and stared up at the ceiling. "Okay, let's get moving," he said, pulling away from her.

I said good-bye to Mel, who was looking a little calmer, and followed the men out the back door. At least it had stopped raining. We covered the distance in about half the time I normally took and I wondered if Dan and Bent were more concerned than they let on. There were no lights on at the gallery, and Dan pulled on the door to make sure it was securely locked, then he knocked, and we waited long enough he was sure nobody was coming.

He held out his hand, and I gave him my keys. We circled around to the side of the building, and Dan reached for the door that led to my apartment. It opened easily. "I thought you said you locked your door."

"I thought I did. I know it was locked when I came home. I may have forgotten when I left."

Dan motioned for Bent and me to take a step back. He inched the door open and disappeared inside. Bent looked at me, shrugged his shoulders, and stepped into the entry. Not willing to stand outside in the cold by myself, I joined him and closed the door behind me. We stood there, staring up the darkened stairway, lit only by the bobbing light of Dan's flashlight above us. We heard him call for Taylor, his footsteps trailing away from us as I assumed he checked the living room and bedroom.

His head appeared at the top of the stairs. "Nobody here."

I turned on the lights, and Dan started back down, switching off his flashlight. "I'm sorry, Dan. I must have left it open after all."

"At least we know she didn't come back here. Let's go check the boat, Bent."

"What if she's not there?" I asked.

"If they aren't there, I'm going home and going to bed. They're adults, Cara. They're not even legally missing until they've been gone forty-eight hours. Trust me, they'll turn up by morning."

"Should I leave the door unlocked in case Tay comes back?"

I watched Dan exchange looks with Bent before he answered. "I don't think she'll come back this late."

He headed outside, and Bent gave me a pat on the shoulder. "Never hurts to have your gun handy."

I wouldn't let myself lock the door behind them. I was not going to let myself live in fear. I shivered in a cold that was more emotional than physical and forced myself up the stairs. I switched off the light and let my eyes adjust to the moonlight. I walked to the window and looked down at the street. I watched while Dan and Bent walked along the boardwalk and disappeared down the steps leading to the pier. Minutes ticked by,

I'm not sure how many, before the shapes reappeared. They turned toward the far end of the road, moving slowly until they were swallowed up in the darkness.

Turning to go to bed, my eyes were drawn to the awning in front of city hall. There was movement, and my heart leaped to my throat when I saw it. Two shoes, attached to two legs, the rest hidden in the shadows. I reeled backward as if I'd been bitten by a snake. I grabbed my cell phone and punched in the number.

"He's out there!" I whispered into the phone.

"Who's out where? Cara? Where are you?"

"I'm here. In the apartment. Dan, he's down there right now. The guy I told you about."

"Stay where you are," Dan's voice snapped with authority. "Stay away from the windows, and don't open the door until I get there."

Remembering I hadn't locked the door, I stumbled down the stairs, tripping over my feet in the dark but managing to keep moving. I threw myself at the door and shoved the dead bolt, relaxing only when I heard it click. I leaned against the door, deliberately slowing my rapid, shallow breaths, willing myself to calm down. Once my heart had stopped drumming out every other sound, I heard a noise. Surely Dan couldn't have made it back so quickly, but I wasn't the best judge of time even when I wasn't scared.

I turned to unlock the door then froze as I heard, more than saw, the doorknob rattle. I backed away, an icy hand gripping my chest that had nothing to do with the cold in the entryway. The knob rattled again, and I heard something thud softly against the door. Stealth mode forgotten, I ran up the stairs in a panic. I ran straight to the bedroom and slammed the door shut. Why hadn't Dad and I thought to put a lock on the bedroom door? With strength I didn't know I had, I shoved my dresser over to block the door.

I dug through my bedside table until my hand struck metal in the darkness. I was shaking fiercely as I struggled to load my handgun and kept dropping bullets onto the floor. *Calm down!* I closed my eyes and tried to breathe. My hands weren't exactly steady when I opened them again, but at least more bullets went into the chamber than onto the floor. I flipped on the safety and sat on the edge of the bed, straining to hear, but picking up nothing but the rush of blood in my ears.

Then I heard music. Where was it coming from? I looked around the room, trying to place the familiar tune, then realized it was coming from my pocket. I forced myself to start breathing again and pulled out my cell phone. It was Dan.

"I'm outside."

"Did you catch him?"

"Nobody's here, Cara."

"But I saw him! And when I went down to lock the door, there was somebody out there. I heard him try to open the door, and when he couldn't, he tried to force it open. Thank God we built that door to withstand a bear."

There was silence for a moment, and I heard him talking to someone. "There's nobody here now. Bent says come on down and you can stay with them tonight."

I'd had more than my share of scares for one night, so I grabbed a change of clothes, shoved my dresser out of the way, and went downstairs. Unlocking the door, I opened it to find Bent waiting on the landing. "Where's Dan?"

"You ready? Be sure you lock up this time."

I pulled the door shut, and Bent tested it. He put his arm around my shoulder and hustled me to the wooden sidewalk. It wasn't until we were inside the warm kitchen, door securely locked behind us, that he told me where Dan had gone. "No sign of your Mr. Shoes, Cara, but we did find footprints leading to your door, then off toward the back of the building."

"Not Tay's?" I had a sick feeling in my stomach and pushed away the cocoa Mel had made for me.

Bent shook his head. "Too big."

"Oh, Cara." Mel's eyes were wide and her face pale.

Bent wrapped his arms around her, rocking her back and forth, his voice low and steady. "It's okay. Cara can stay with us till the season's over, then she'll be home with your folks."

Watching them, it hit me. How could I have missed the signs? Mel's eyes were closed, her head resting on Bent's chest, her body leaning against his. Bent saw the question in my eyes and smiled. I did some quick math and came up with February. A Valentine's baby sounded just about perfect.

Chapter 6

The sound of the shower woke me up. I lay in my
bed, warm under a down comforter, listening to the
water and wondering why Taylor was up so early. I
persuaded one eye to open and looked around the dark
bedroom. Something wasn't right. Either my bed was in
the wrong spot, or the window was on the wrong side of
the room. I succeeded in getting my other eye open and
remembered I wasn't in my apartment at all.

I was tempted to pull the comforter over my head
and stay in Mel's guest room all morning, but I knew I
couldn't do that. I had a business to run, and there
would be time to sleep late when the season ended. The
last week of the season is always great for sales because
cruisers know shop owners would rather sell than store
their inventory. I don't mark down my prices like other
merchants since I ship unsold work back to the artist
when the season ends, but somehow the end of the
season had always brought me better than average sales
just the same.

In one motion, I threw off the comforter and swung
my legs over the side of the bed, letting the shock of the
cold air wake me up. Everyone has a theory whether
it's better to ease out of bed on cold mornings or just
jump right out and let the cold hit you all at once. I'd
heard enough of the debates helping Mel out the first
year they opened the restaurant to know that nobody
had a good answer. If I could afford it, I'd just keep my
house warm enough that there wasn't any cold to adjust
to, but Alaskan heating bills were enough to give you a

heart attack already. No need to compound the damage by keeping the house as warm overnight as you do during the day.

It was still dark, and it would stay dark for another few hours. The closer we got to winter, the longer the darkness would last and the more fleeting the light would become. Living in twilight is something you adjust to, or you don't. It's probably harder on outsiders than adjusting to the cold. Even in a town full of hermits, we're all just a little more so in the wintertime.

Freshly showered and dressed, hair combed and teeth brushed, I made my way down to the kitchen where Mel was pulling out ingredients for today's breakfast. She'd had enough time to get a pot of coffee going while I was in the shower, and the aroma was heavenly. I poured myself a mug and leaned against the counter, watching her graceful movements and letting the caffeine burn off the rest of the fog in my brain. "When were you going to tell me?"

Mel's face flushed, but she continued working. "When the season ended."

"You're gonna be a great mom."

Mel put down the spoon she'd been using. Tears threatened, but she blinked them away. "I can't even imagine how I'm going to manage next season."

"Bring the baby down and turn her loose in the dining room."

Mel laughed and wiped her eyes, getting flour on her cheek. "Yeah, I'm sure that'll work."

"You wait and see. The whole town will adopt this baby. We're not exactly overrun with babies around here. Besides, I am gonna be an amazing aunt."

"You'd better be."

"Are you planning to have the baby at home or go to Juneau?" Coho Bay doesn't have a doctor even during the season. We have a shiny new clinic, built with cruise ship taxes, but the city fathers have yet to attract a doctor to staff it.

"Home if we can." Mel poured batter into muffin tins as she talked. "Gabby says so far, so good."

Gabby Lighthorse had been delivering babies around Coho Bay for almost twenty years. She'd trained with the midwife who'd delivered me when I was born. She was certified by the state, but that's not why women trusted Gabby. She cared deeply about every mother and every child she helped usher into the world. Most women could safely deliver at home, but Gabby made sure that if anything could complicate a delivery, those moms went to Juneau where they could be cared for by an OB-GYN and deliver in a hospital.

"Is this why you've been after me to stay in town this winter?" I finished my coffee and put the mug in the dishwasher, then ran hot water into the sink.

"I always want you to stay in town, Cara."

"But with the baby coming…"

"All right, fine. With the baby coming, I really want to have you nearby. Happy now? I want Mom and Dad to stay too. I'm going to ask when they get back."

"You won't have to ask Mom. She's not gonna let herself be five miles away when her first grandbaby is born. She'll probably send Dad home to pack and move right in as soon as you tell her the news. Don't envy you having her that nearby."

Mel stopped what she was doing and stared at me. "I hadn't thought of that."

"Tell you what I'll do. They can have my apartment, and I'll stay in the guest room. Won't be much sleeping in that room once the baby gets there, but I'll make it work."

"The baby can sleep in our room."

"So what are we looking at, five months?"

"The time is going to fly by." Mel slid the muffin tins into the oven. "It's sweet of you to offer, but if I know our mother, she won't go for being all the way down at your place."

"It's two blocks away."

"Two blocks too far. You'll see. I don't like the idea of you being alone though. What about Taylor? Is she determined to move out to the island, or could we get her to stay with you?"

Elbow-deep in dishwater, last night's fear swept over me. My knees buckled, and I found myself sitting on the floor, dripping suds all over the legs of my jeans. Mel rushed over and crouched beside me. The look on my face must have really been something because she looked up at the ceiling and yelled, "Bent, get down here!"

He arrived moments later, jeans on but no shirt, his face covered in shaving cream. He slid onto the floor beside us, his eyes scanning Mel for injury or distress. "Baby, what is it?" he asked, his voice sounding about three pitches higher than normal. "What happened?"

I shook myself back into the present. "I'm fine. She's fine. It's okay, really."

Mel grabbed one elbow, Bent took the other, and together they pulled me to my feet. "Cara, are you all right?" asked Mel. Her breath was coming fast, and her face was pale.

"I'm fine. I'm sorry. I don't know what came over me, but I'm fine now, really. Please don't worry, Mel." She relaxed her iron grip on my arm, and color began to return to her cheeks.

"What happened?" asked Bent. The crisis past, his disheveled appearance must have struck Mel as funny because she started to giggle. She tried several times to stop, but she kept on giggling, and Bent's efforts to sooth her only made it worse. She sat down on one of the stools and struggled to regain her composure.

"I'm sorry, honey. Honestly, I'm okay." She batted him away. "Don't fuss."

"You're the one who yelled for me to get down here. You scared the crap outta me. Can somebody tell me what's wrong?"

"It's my fault," I said. "I was so excited about the baby that I wasn't thinking about last night, and then Mel mentioned Taylor and all of a sudden—Wham!"

"Bent, honey, finish getting ready. I'll fill you in later." Shaving cream dripped from his face and splatted onto his chest. I bit my lip to keep from laughing because I knew it would set Mel off again. Bent looked at me, and I had to look away. I heard him sigh and retreat up the stairs.

Once he was out of earshot, Mel picked up our conversation. "This is why I don't think you should be in that apartment alone, Cara. Don't tell me you aren't scared."

"Okay, I'm scared, but I've got no good reason to be. The one you should be worried about is Taylor. Can you imagine her on the island all by herself this winter?"

"Not really. Can she even get a cell signal out there? What if something breaks down? I can't picture Taylor being able to fix it."

"She has a ham radio, and she might be a decent handyman. Who knew she could work a table saw, but she did just fine? It's her emotional health I'm worried about. How's she going to take being out there without Johnny?"

"Taylor isn't my sister. Now, I don't care what Dan says, this Mr. Shoes is not a figment of your imagination. Your imagination didn't create those footprints."

I steadied myself against the counter, finding the solid surface comforting. "Maybe it was Frank, checking to make sure I locked the door."

"Then where is he, Cara? Where is he, and where is Taylor?"

"I don't know, but it's Coho Bay, Mel. I'm sure they're fine, and I'm sure we've gotten ourselves all worked up over nothing."

Mel frowned. "Pregnancy hormones?"

"I don't think that excuse will work for me. How about sympathy hormones?"

Mel snickered and stood up. "Hormones or no hormones, if I don't get moving, I'll be stuck with a dining room full of people and nothing but coffee to serve them."

It was still dark, so I borrowed a flashlight when I left for the gallery. I felt a little silly with the flashlight in my left hand and my right resting on the gun in my coat pocket, but I had enough memory of the fear I'd felt last night not to let that stop me. I checked my apartment before I went to the gallery to see if Taylor had returned. The door was locked, and when I opened it and called her name, there was no response. I shone my flashlight at the stoop but saw no trace of the footprints Bent and Dan had found the night before.

Once in the gallery, I leaned heavily on the door, forcing it closed against the protest of the hydraulic arm. Once I was able to lock it behind me, I started shaking. The strength went out of my legs, and for the second time that morning, I found myself sinking helplessly to the floor. This time I didn't have to be brave for Mel, so I closed my eyes, leaned back against the cold glass of the door, and rode the wave. I'm not very good at handling strong emotion, and this business was stirring up emotions I couldn't even describe. The harder I told myself there was nothing to be afraid of, the more my hands shook until I couldn't grip the flashlight anymore. It wasn't that I'd never been afraid before. You can't hunt without fear, because no matter what kind of game you're after, you can bet there's something bigger out there hunting you. The tables can turn quickly as they had for Johnny. Just that fast, your life can be over. When you live close to nature, you learn to live with that kind of danger. You don't like it, but you don't let it keep you from doing what you need to do.

This was an entirely different brand of fear, and I didn't know how to stare it down. Frank had frightened me with his late-night panic attack, and it hadn't been my imagination that someone had tried to get in, and I didn't think they were selling cookies. Now Taylor and Frank had vanished, and I didn't care what Dan said. It wasn't like her to take off like that. For all I knew there could be a two-legged predator on the hunt in Coho Bay, and Dan wasn't doing anything to stop him. Animals follow certain patterns of behavior, but people are far less predictable. I'd rather stare down a pack of wolves than a single murderous human.

With these thoughts simmering in my mind, there was a knock at the door against which I was leaning. It probably isn't possible for me to have leaped in one motion from where I had been sitting to a standing position facing the door, but that's what my brain told me I did. I crouched into my best imitation of an attack position I'd seen in a hundred movies and brandished the flashlight like a weapon. How I would have stopped an attacker with a flashlight and why I didn't reach into my coat pocket for my actual weapon is a mystery, but it's probably best that my gun stayed where it was.

My would-be assassin yelped and jumped away from the door, her hand coming up to protect her eyes from the light. I couldn't see her from the glare of the light reflecting back at me in the glass, but I could hear her with crystal clarity. Her first words gave me another lesson in profanity, but she finished with, "Cara! Cut the light!"

I lowered the beam and twisted the lock open, grabbing her arm and pulling her inside. "Where on earth have you been, Tay? You scared me half to death taking off like that."

She rubbed her arm. "What is your problem? The apartment was locked, and I was too mad to go back for the key. Why were you sitting in the doorway? You scared the life out of me jumping up like that."

"Never mind what I was doing. Where did you go last night?"

She walked past me. "I need coffee."

I followed, my steps slow but my mind racing. I'd been asking a lot of questions lately and not getting many answers. It was beginning to get on my nerves. "Where did you go?"

"I was standing on the stoop, trying to decide what to do when I saw Frank. He asked me what I was doing and when I told him, he offered to…" Measuring coffee into the filter suddenly claimed her complete attention, and a terrible truth flooded over me.

"You did not. You seriously did not." There was no answer, but I could see I'd struck the nail right on the head. "Taylor Louise Snow, how could you?"

She flipped the switch on the coffeemaker and wheeled to face me, defiance radiating from every pore. "Why the hell not?"

I was speechless. A million words blew through my head, but my lips couldn't seem to form them. A whirlwind engulfed me—anger, jealousy, betrayal— and I fought to control it. I turned away from her, crossed to my desk, and switched on my computer. I stared unseeingly at the screen, waiting for it to come alive. It was as though the onslaught of emotion had short-circuited something in me, and I found myself feeling nothing at all.

"That's it? You have nothing more to say?"

I sat back in my chair, sorting through all of the things I felt like saying to see if there was something I actually could. Words tumbled over themselves to get out, but I stopped them. What was the point?

Taylor bustled around the room, talking quickly as she pulled mugs out of the cupboard. "I never said I was gonna marry the guy. He was just... there." She put creamer in my mug and sugar in her own. Her arm shook as she poured the coffee. "I miss him, Cara."

My anger was compounded by guilt. It was Saturday. The first anniversary of Johnny's death had to be hell for her. Who was I to give her crap for taking comfort wherever she found it? There was no sense being angry with her for sleeping with Frank. It was done, and it couldn't be undone even if she regretted it. I felt a sharp pang about Frank, but I pushed it aside. As I'd done so many times before, I reminded myself that if a man had been genuinely interested in me, he wouldn't have slept with her. The tiny door in my heart that had opened when he'd looked at me, slammed shut.

Taylor brought my coffee. "I'm sorry you were worried. I should have left a note. I wasn't thinking straight." She sat down and stared into her cup. "I'm so raw right now. Everything hurts."

"I need to call Mel." Words were still elusive, but I managed to get that much out. I was hurt and angry and probably a few other things I didn't stop to analyze, but at least with this I was on familiar, if unwelcome, ground.

"Let me," said Taylor, digging her cell phone out of her purse. "I could kick myself, getting her all worked up at a time like this."

"Did Mel tell you about the baby?"

Taylor rolled her eyes at me as she waited for Mel to pick up. "A woman doesn't have to tell you something like that."

I bit my lip to keep from pointing out that if she'd answered her phone last night she would have saved us all a lot of worry. I felt sick listening to her speaking with such earnest contrition to Mel, and without warning, I heard my mother's voice. *You'll eat yourself alive from the inside if you don't tell a person how you feel.* Of course, she only said that after I'd given in to whatever strange demand she'd made on me, but she did have a point. Mel told me I ought to have "Welcome" tattooed on my forehead if I were going to be a doormat all my life.

It wasn't fair. I hated confrontation, and I shouldn't have to fight for what I needed from people who were supposed to be my friends. People who loved you should want for you what you want for yourself. You shouldn't have to watch your back around someone if she was truly your friend. I closed my eyes and pushed the thought away. I had work to do, and I didn't have time to examine Taylor's motives.

I sat up at my computer and started printing shipping labels. By the time Kenny arrived, my mind was clear again and I had the shipment ready for him. "Could you pick me up a fuel filter for Dad's boat? I've been meaning to ask you."

"Another one? He's got bigger problems than the fuel filter if that last one went bad already."

"I know. Crazy, huh? They'll have to tear the motor apart Thursday. Hopefully we won't be asking you for more parts."

"Hope not. Bent can't afford to be without a boat with Mel in the family way." Had everybody known about the baby but me? I've got to work on my powers of observation. Kenny hopped in his van and chugged down the street. Taylor and I spent the next hour pulling the last of the artwork out of the back room. With only two more ships coming, I wanted to be sure every single piece had an opportunity to be seen and sold. When we finished, she went upstairs to shower and change. I walked through the gallery, allowing myself to absorb the peace I always felt being surrounded by beautiful work. My degree is in business, and I love using what I learned to make the gallery a success, but I get so caught up in the business end of things that I forget how much the art inspires me.

I paused in front of Johnny's paintings and remembered the last time I'd seen him. He'd come into the gallery with Taylor the morning he died. He wanted to see how many paintings I had left, and she wanted to take advantage of the open weather to spend a day in town. It was a busy day, and she'd offered to help, so Johnny had set out alone with his sketchpad. I hadn't spared him another thought until Kenny had shown up at the front door, bursting with the news. I hadn't wanted to believe him, but when Dan walked in a few minutes later, it was written in every line in his face. He'd taken Taylor into the back room, his eyes locking with mine over her shoulders, filling me with dread.

My first thought when Dan emerged had been to close the gallery and go to her, but he told me she didn't want to see anybody. I'd started to push past him, but he'd put his hands on my shoulders and told me to let her be. It had felt wrong to go about business as usual in the gallery. Johnny had been my friend too, and I was reeling with the shock of losing him, but I put my own feelings on hold and did what I thought was best for Taylor. I don't know if I let her down by not going to her. We never talk about that day.

I wondered what Dan had wanted to talk to Taylor about the other day and why Johnny's estate was still unsettled. More questions to add to the list of ones she hadn't answered. Johnny's estate should have been simple. The money in the marriage had been Taylor's. Johnny hadn't brought much more than the island and his paintings into the marriage. Even with the staggering demand for his work after his death, the amount I'd deposited into the estate account was a drop in the bucket to the fortune Taylor's parents had left her when they'd died. I wondered what was causing the holdup.

Chapter 7

The dining room at Mel's was quiet that night. Many of the locals would be leaving Coho Bay at the end of the week, heading to winter homes spread out along the rugged coast or scattered in clearings throughout the woods. They ate quickly, talked in muted tones, and left without dessert to begin packing up their summer cabins. The seasonal workers who hadn't left when school started had commandeered two tables along the far wall. Their voices were animated as they exchanged cell phone numbers and social media handles. I wondered how many of them would keep the promise to stay in touch.

I absorbed all of this without looking up from my plate. There could have been a marching band behind me, and it wouldn't have torn me away from my dinner. Bent had made meatloaf sandwiches from the last of the moose, and Bent's meatloaf was a culinary masterpiece, worthy of my undivided attention. He had mixed in leftover elk sausage, and the combination was heavenly. Nestled beside it was a small pile of Bent's homemade chips, liberally spiced with barbeque rub. I don't think Mel married him for his cooking, but in my opinion that would have been enough.

I hoped Dad had found time to scout a few promising hunting spots while he was doing the count. We'd drawn both moose and elk this year, and I was anxious to escape the bustle of the season for the peace of the woods. Hunting with my father was the highlight of my year. From sighting in our rifles to packing up the four-wheelers to stalking the herd as silently as we could, it was a week of pure enjoyment. Mom and Mel had come with us only once before proclaiming it too cold, dirty, and smelly for their tastes. After that, they holed up in the cabin canning, freezing, and drying the late harvest from my parents' garden. That kind of work didn't appeal to me, and the fact that they enjoyed it made me a little concerned about their sanity. Bent was coming with us this year, so we hoped to bring home enough meat to have a steak or two left for the end of the season celebration next year.

Perched on the stool beside me, Taylor picked at her food, then shoved her plate away. "How can you eat like that?"

She caught me mid-chew, so I swallowed before I answered. "I thought you liked moose loaf."

"I wasn't talking about the food."

I watched as she turned her paper napkin into confetti. I was trying not to let the little green monster get me. Taylor had been collecting other women's boyfriends for years, making her decidedly unpopular in college. I'd seen it happen enough times to know that it wasn't so much that Taylor went after men, but that she didn't turn down what they were offering. Taylor had told me once that any man who could be stolen wasn't a man you'd want to keep. "I'm doing her a favor," she told me once when I'd called her on it. "Just think if she'd married him and then he'd been unfaithful. This way at least she doesn't have kids with the jerk."

I doubted our former friend had felt that way about it, but while she'd put all the blame on Taylor, I'd been at that party and I'd seen him come onto her. She should have walked away; he was the one who'd made the commitment, and it had been his choice to break it. Taylor had known I was interested in Frank, and if he made the first move, she could have ducked it, but I had no claim on the man. I couldn't even blame Frank for turning to Taylor since I'd pretty much ignored him all summer. He had my attention now, going all superhero on Jack, but I had deflected his attentions even then. If I was alone now, it was nobody's fault but my own.

I finished my sandwich and picked up the conversation. "So what did you mean?"

"Frank."

"What about him?" I asked as though I hadn't just been thinking about him.

"He said he'd meet us for dinner."

"He's usually here, but I wouldn't call that meeting us for dinner."

"Well this time he said it specifically. He was going to finish his last tour, go home and take a shower, then meet us here after the gallery closed."

I grinned at Mel when she set a dish of apple crumble in front of me. My favorite. I spared only part of my brain for Taylor. The rest of me reveled in warm apples, cinnamon, and granola. "Frank was gonna take a shower? Must have been trying to impress you."

"He likes you. He just doesn't think you like him."

I finished my dessert and stared at her. "He has sex with you, then says I'm the one he's really after. I bet that happens all the time."

"You could have had him anytime this summer. Don't blame me if a man gets tired of waiting."

I opened my mouth to retort but shut it firmly. Taking my silence as agreement, Taylor continued. "If you're done stuffing yourself, can we go?"

"Don't go getting all snarky with me, or I'll forget how glad I was to see you this morning." I didn't think she was sorry, but at least she had the decency to appear contrite, so I slid off my barstool and went into the kitchen to let Mel and Bent know where we were going.

"Do you have your gun with you?" asked Bent.

"In my coat pocket. I came to borrow your flashlight again."

Mel retrieved it. "Call me every fifteen minutes."

"Sheesh, Mel, you sound more like Mom every minute. Must be the hormones."

"Don't be mean."

Taylor was waiting for me by the door, coat and gloves on, arms crossed, and right leather boot tapping. I handed her the flashlight and shrugged into my own coat, checking to make sure my handgun was still in the pocket and on safety. Taylor set off toward the marina at a blistering pace. "Hey, Cara, let's start with the boat," I mumbled sarcastically, but she was already too far ahead to hear.

She waited at the bottom of the steps for me to catch up before striking out toward where the commercial boats were docked. Coho Bay boasted a small fleet of excursion boats, enough to handle an army of cruisers. Frank's boat, Whale of a Time, was tied up five slips from the end. Taylor scrambled up the ladder and hopped onto the deck. Listening to her calling for him, it struck me how far we were from where Dad's boat was tied up. Private boats were on the other side of the marina at least a hundred yards away. I wondered how Frank could have heard us trying to get the motor started.

"He's not here." I looked up to see her climb down the ladder at a much more sedate pace than she had gone up.

"I didn't think he would be. Let's go check his cabin."

She joined me on the pier, walking slowly this time. "If you didn't think he'd be at the boat, you should have said something and saved us a trip."

"Seriously? You were halfway to the marina while I was still putting my coat on."

She ignored me. "Poke your head in at Mel's, will you? See if he got there late."

I did, but he hadn't, so we set off up the road that led out of town. My parents owned several cabins that they rented out, one of which Frank had been living in all season. They were dry cabins, meaning they had no running water. They had composting toilets and access to a well for drinking water and personal hygiene, though they had to heat the water on a wood stove for cooking and bathing. There were camp showers set up outside the few cabins that were still occupied. It was rustic, but dry cabins weren't uncommon in rural Alaska.

The cabins were just over a mile out of town, so we quickened our pace to stay warm and spoke loudly to discourage bears and other nocturnal residents. We talked about nothing important, more to be making noise than conversation. By the time we got to Frank's, I was out of breath. The cabin was dark, but Taylor didn't hesitate. She walked right up and pounded on the door. When he didn't answer, she pounded on the door again, kicking it a few times for good measure.

"Cripes, Tay. Don't break the door down."

My cell rang, and I pulled it out, hoping it was Frank telling us to cut it out, but it was Mel. "Cara, where are you?"

"Frank's place. Did I miss my check-in, mother hen?"

"He's not there?"

"Nope. Tay's just about knocked the door off its hinges, but nobody's home."

I heard her talking to someone away from the phone then Dan's voice came on the line. "Cara, you two wait there. I'll be right out."

"Dan? What's the matter?"

"Don't touch anything, and don't go inside the cabin."

"I can't go in. I didn't bring my key. What's going on?"

"Just sit tight."

He hung up, and I stood staring at Taylor, who by this time had given up trying to beat down the door. I'm sure the one renter I had left in the cabins would appreciate that. "What was that all about?"

"I don't know, but we're gonna find out. Dan's on his way."

"Dan? Why? Did something happen to Frank?"

"I just told you I don't know."

She slumped against the porch railing and asked no more questions. I paced and stamped my feet, hugging my arms to my body to ward off the cold. Fifteen minutes after he called, Dan pulled up in front of the cabin. I walked over to meet him. "What's up, Dan?"

"No sign of Frank?"

"No. What's up? Why'd you come running out here?"

He didn't answer. Instead, he fished something out of his pocket and handed it to me. It was Mel's passkey. Her keychain had a tiny mixer on it. Mine had the tip of an elk antler. "Let's take a look." Dan climbed down and started toward the cabin. He nodded at Taylor, who ignored him, and waited for me. "Don't have a search warrant. As the property manager, you need to open it and give me permission to enter."

"When did you start going by the book?" He didn't answer, so I unlocked the door. Before I could open it, Dan took hold of my arm and gently pushed me back.

"Let me go first, Cara." There was something in his voice I hadn't heard before, and the chill that ran through me wasn't because of the night air. "You ladies wait here." He went inside, closing the door behind him. I heard the lock click.

The light came on, so I moved to the window, but the shade was down. Dan's shadow moved through the one-room cabin, but I couldn't see what he was doing. Taylor was standing on the edge of the porch, staring up into the cloudless sky. The door opened, and the light went off. "Find anything?" I asked.

Dan shook his head. "You two must be half-frozen. Let me give you a ride back."

Taylor didn't respond, so I accepted for both of us. I waited until we were on our way, me seated in the middle with Dan's heater on high. "Why all the cloak and dagger? Is something wrong?"

"I hear you two were together last night, Ms. Lennon." I nudged Dan when Taylor didn't answer. "I'm not calling her a name that isn't hers! She can talk to me in jail if she doesn't like it."

"Not that it's any of your business," said Taylor, "but yes, we were together at his cabin. He walked me into town this morning."

"Why didn't you answer the door last night?"

Taylor stared out the window, and the truck slowed. I guess Dan wasn't going to get us into town until he got some answers. Taylor must have realized it too. "We were... busy... when you knocked."

The air in the truck felt heavy. Why, oh why did I have to be stuck in the middle of this conversation? "Where did he go after he dropped you off?" Dan asked, pulling up in front of Mel's.

"I have no idea." Taylor opened the door and started to climb out.

"Then you don't know if the body we fished out of the bay is Frank?"

Taylor spun around to face him, openmouthed. She stumbled backward, and I grabbed her arm to keep her from falling. She stammered but didn't seem to be able to form a cohesive sentence.

"Good Lord, Dan, why didn't you say something?" My heart was in my throat, but I managed to speak for both of us.

"I asked you a question, Ms. Lennon." Dan's voice was colder than an Alaskan winter.

"My God, no! It can't be Frank." Taylor started shaking, and I held on to her, shoving my own feelings away.

"You can be a real jerk, Dan." I scooted over in the seat, glaring back at him. His face was unreadable in the shadows. "Is it Frank or isn't it?"

Much to my relief Mel and Bent came rushing out. Bent scooped Taylor up. Partly carrying her, partly helping her walk, he got her inside. I slid out, and Mel threw her arms around me. "Oh Cara, isn't it horrible?"

"Supercop over there won't give me a straight answer," I said, pulling away from her. "Was it Frank?"

Mel slammed the passenger door and walked with me into the restaurant. "They don't know for sure. It's a man, but his head..." She turned positively green.

I stumbled, and Mel put her arm around me. I fought to keep my voice steady. "Mel, don't think about it. You don't need this kind of stress right now."

The place was empty. When Dan came in looking for Taylor, the tables had cleared as locals rushed out to see whatever there might have been to see. Bent had closed up early and waited for Dan to bring us home. A local crabber had been checking his pots and pulled up a body of a man. The head and hands had been cut off, so there was only speculation that it might be Frank based on the fact that he was the only one unaccounted for.

"It might not be him, Tay." I took both her hands in mine and forced her to make eye contact. "They can't possibly know yet whether anyone else is missing." It would be cold comfort if Frank was okay, only to have some other local family devastated by the loss, but it was all the hope I could give Taylor right now.

"State police are on their way." Four sets of eyes turned toward Dan. "DNA will tell us if it's Frank."

"It could be anybody, Dan," I said.

"When was the last time you saw him?"

"Dinner last night, but I'm sure people have seen him since then."

Dan nodded toward Taylor. "Ms. Lennon said he dropped her off at the gallery this morning. Nobody else has seen him today."

"It was a cruise ship day. He must've done his tours." I looked from Dan to Mel to Bent, but one shook his head and the other two just looked sad. "He no-showed on his tours?"

"Looks that way."

"Mel, didn't Frank come in for breakfast after he dropped Tay off?" She shook her head, and I swung around to face Dan. "Something must've happened to him between the gallery and here because you know that's where he would have been heading. Why are you just standing there? Why aren't you out doing whatever it is cops do at a time like this?"

Dan didn't flinch. "What would you suggest, Cara? Look for your mythical Mr. Shoes?"

"He's not mythical! You saw his footprints outside my door last night."

"There was somebody there, Dan," agreed Bent, and I flashed him a smile.

"I can't find the killer until I confirm the identity of the victim."

"How long will that take?"

"Weeks, maybe. Depends on how busy they are up at the state lab."

"Weeks? The killer will be long gone by then!" I heard the hint of hysteria in my voice, but I was having a hard time fighting it.

Dan's eyes softened, and he put a gentle hand on my shoulder. To my surprise my nerves began to calm. "Neighbors are out checking on neighbors to see if anyone else is missing. I should know by morning, and if Frank is still the only one we haven't found, I'll move forward on the assumption the body is his. Better?"

I nodded, and he took a step toward Taylor. "If it is Frank, who had a motive to kill him?" There were unshed tears in Taylor's eyes, but she didn't answer.

"Do you know how he died, Dan?" asked Bent.

"You know I can't talk about an open investigation."

"The body was found by a fisherman. Every gory detail will be all over town by morning."

Dan sighed. We all knew how quickly the gossip mill worked in Coho Bay. "I couldn't tell. May have been shot in the head, but I couldn't say for sure."

"What kind of person cuts up a body and hauls it out to the bay?" asked Mel, looking queasy.

"A sick son of a—"

Dan cut me off. "Would take some strength."

"And maybe more than one person," added Bent.

"With a boat, though half the town has a boat," I said.

"And the other half could borrow one," agreed Bent.

"If it were me, I'd use Frank's boat," said Mel, and we all looked at her in surprise. "I'm just saying, you wouldn't want to risk the police finding evidence on your own boat."

"Good point," said Dan. "I'll have the state lab boys take a look tomorrow."

"Taylor didn't notice anything wrong on Frank's boat tonight, did you, Tay?" She shook her head, her eyes large.

"Is that so?" Dan sat down next to Taylor, who shifted her chair back, putting a little distance between them. "What were you doing on Frank's boat, Ms. Lennon?"

"Looking for Frank, of course," I said when she didn't answer.

Dan kept his eyes on Taylor. "Wouldn't it have been more likely he was at home?"

Taylor twisted the leather gloves in her lap but didn't answer. This one I couldn't help her with because I was also curious why she'd headed for the boat. Dan looked up at me. "You see Frank this morning?"

"No," I admitted, drawing out the word into one long syllable.

"So we only have her word for it that he was still alive."

He was clearly insinuating she knew more than she did, and why Taylor didn't speak up to defend herself was beyond me. If someone were hinting I'd killed a man and chopped up his body, I'd be hopping mad. Since she said nothing, I jumped in. "Whoever did this would be covered in blood, don't you think? Taylor turned up before dawn wearing the same clothes she'd had on the night before. I would have noticed if she'd had blood all over them."

"Brava!" Mel clapped. "You sound just like a TV show, Cara."

"Thanks!"

Dan held up his hands. "I never said I thought Ms. Lennon killed Frank. I'm just trying to nail down the last time he was seen. Not a lot of people up and about that time of day who might have seen him."

"Kenny!" I said, snapping my fingers. "Kenny was about half an hour after Taylor, but he could have been making other stops before he got to the gallery."

"Good point, Cara," said Dan, standing. "I'll catch him before he leaves tomorrow."

Taylor's head snapped up, and her eyes flashed at Dan. "Go ahead and say it. You think I killed Frank because you think I killed Johnny."

"Tay, nobody thinks you killed Johnny."

"He does." She nodded her head at Dan, who was matching her glare for glare.

"No he doesn't, do you, Dan?"

Dan never took his eyes off Taylor. "In case you people have forgotten, this isn't a TV show. There's a real body and a real killer. Everybody's a suspect until I can prove otherwise. Ms. Lennon, I'd like to examine the clothes you were wearing."

"Dan! Tay, you don't have to give him anything."

"Innocent people don't withhold things from the police, Cara."

"Innocent people get railroaded all the time," I said, immediately regretting it when I saw his pained expression. "I'm sorry. I didn't mean you would do something like that."

Dan turned to Taylor. "You're under no obligation to surrender your clothes or to allow me to search for anything else that may become evidence. I would appreciate your cooperation, but I am not in a position to compel it."

"Take the clothes." Taylor spit out the words. "I don't care." She stood up and marched out of the restaurant, Dan following a step behind her.

I handed Mel her passkey, gave her a quick hug, and hurried out the door. I had to run to catch up since Taylor was walking as though she were in training for the Olympics. I unlocked the door, and she stomped up the stairs and into the bedroom. Dan followed her, and I stood in the doorway, leaning against the jam, watching the scene that unfolded. Muttering to herself, Taylor upended the dirty clothes hamper onto the bed and started digging through it.

Dan stood beside the bed, hands on his waist, one resting lightly on the gun that was holstered there. I wondered if he was doing that because he thought Taylor might have a weapon hidden among the socks and sweaters or if it was just habit. It was a bit of a shock to me to realize I didn't know Dan well enough to know the answer.

"Here, take them." A blouse and a pair of jeans flew at Dan. He folded them methodically, then pulled a bag from his pocket, tucked the clothes inside, and sealed it.

"Since when do you carry evidence bags?" I asked as I walked back down the stairs with him.

"Since somebody pulled a body from the bay." He stopped at the front door and looked back up the stairs. He motioned me to follow him outside. It was cold on the stoop, and I found myself wishing I hadn't taken my coat off. "I know she's your friend, Cara, but this is the second man she's been with who ended up dead."

"Dan..."

"I'm just saying you should be careful." I stood watching him disappear around the building, headed not to his truck but the city offices across the street. Taylor was waiting for me in the mudroom when I went back inside.

"What were you two talking about?" Her arms were crossed over her chest, and her tone was hostile.

"He reminded me there's a murderer on the loose, so I should be careful. Like I needed reminding."

"What else did he say?"

"Isn't that enough?" She gave me a long look, but with Dan's warning ringing in my ears, I didn't volunteer more. She turned and went back up the stairs.

"I'm taking a shower."

I heard the bedroom door slam and a few minutes later, heard water hitting the shower wall. I walked slowly up the stairs and dropped onto the couch. The accumulated stress of the past two days was making my head hurt. No matter what Dan said, it was impossible to think of Taylor as some kind of black widow. I knew she'd loved Johnny, and there'd been no mistaking her devastation when she saw his body. I didn't know how Frank managed to end up in a crab pot in the bay, but there was no way Taylor could have done that. Even if she could have, why would she have wanted to kill Frank, a guy she'd slept with only the night before? She'd seemed genuinely shaken when Dan told us the news, and I'd never known her to be a convincing actress.

On the other hand, she'd been lying to me and avoiding my questions ever since she came back. I slumped over on the couch, too tired to wait for her to get out of the shower so I could go to bed. As much as I wanted to believe her, my guard was up whether I wanted it to be or not.

Chapter 8

I slept fitfully, dreaming of Taylor standing over a headless corpse, brandishing a butcher knife that was dripping with blood. She was laughing, but her eyes were cold. She took a step toward me, and I woke, sitting straight up and breathing so fast the room was spinning. It was still dark and quiet, but my internal clock told me it was time to force myself off the couch and into the shower. I threw off the down comforter Taylor must have covered me with last night. Her actual thoughtfulness was in stark contrast to the terrifying image conjured up in my dream.

"Remind me to punch Dan in the nose next time I see him," I said to no one in particular.

The floor was cold under my bare feet as I padded to the bedroom. Taylor must have taken off my shoes for me too. I had to have been out cold if she'd been able to do that without waking me. I knocked lightly on the bedroom door before opening it. She was sprawled out on the bed, and from the condition of the bedding, I'd say she hadn't slept very peacefully either. I gently eased clothes out of my dresser and slipped into the bathroom. I couldn't muffle the sound of the shower, but I made it a quick one and got dressed before switching off the light and opening the bathroom door.

Taylor had rolled over, but otherwise there was no indication I'd disturbed her. I tiptoed back to the living room and found my shoes sitting next to the couch. I thought about waking her, but decided to let her sleep. There was no cruise ship today since the line that normally visited on Sundays had already sent its ship south. I needed to help Mel get breakfast started then get my shipment ready for Kenny, but otherwise, there was nothing I had to do.

The kitchen door was locked when I got to Mel's, but the light was on, so I knocked. "Mel, it's me. Open the door."

I heard the lock click, and the door opened. My sister's worried face peered around the door, looking down at me as I stepped into the warm kitchen. "Why'd you lock me out? It's freezing out there. Feels like it's gonna snow."

"Sorry, my hands were dirty."

I hung up my coat and grabbed an apron. Mel locked the door and went back to her muffins. There weren't many dirty dishes yet, so I joined her at the worktable, warm mug of coffee thawing out my fingers. "There's nothing to be afraid of."

"Who says I'm afraid?"

"You're beating the heck out of those muffins, and they never hurt a soul."

Mel's hand stilled. She looked down at the batter, then pushed the bowl away. "How can you be so calm?"

I took the bowl and ladled batter into the tins Mel had prepared. "Oven hot?"

"Yes, it's ready when you are." She sat down on a metal stool and took a deep breath. "Thanks, Cara. Between morning sickness and all this with Frank and Taylor, I don't know how I'm gonna get through the day. Thank God it's just locals."

"I'll come back once I've got my shipment out and keep you company." I finished with the batter and carefully slid the muffin tins into the oven. I set the timer and went back to the worktable to clean up.

"Anybody left at the cabins?"

"Just one. I've also got a few houses on the far side turning over and Tay's of course." Our family didn't own all those properties, but since I was accustomed to dealing with renters for our cabins, other families trusted me to rent out their properties when they flew south for the summer. The money I earned had been enough to tide me over in the days before the gallery opened. Now that I didn't need the income, I kept doing it because no one else had volunteered to take over the responsibility.

"Did Taylor say anything when you two got home?"

"Nope." I pulled a jug of orange juice out of the cooler and poured a glass for Mel. "I had a nightmare about it though, straight out of a slasher movie."

Mel raised her eyebrows. "You think Taylor had something to do with Frank's death?"

"No, I don't. Dan put the fear of God into me last night." I put the orange juice back and leaned on the counter. "You know Tay. She can be a flake."

"And self-centered."

"And she has a temper, but none of that makes her a killer."

"I suppose anyone could kill if they had reason."

"Tay wouldn't have had any reason to kill Frank. Assuming the body actually is Frank's."

"It has to be, Cara. I don't like it either, but Frank wouldn't blow off his tours."

I stared into my coffee. I felt a tear tip out from the corner of my eye. "I don't want it to be Frank."

"I know."

I put down my cup. "This is crazy. I don't want Frank to be dead, but even if he's alive, he's into Taylor now. I really know my way around men, don't I? First Johnny, now Frank, and that's not even counting the guys in college. Everybody wants Taylor. Nobody wants me."

"Johnny?"

I turned away from her. "It's nothing. I'm feeling sorry for myself. It'll pass."

"I never knew there was something between you and Johnny."

I laughed, but it was one of those times you aren't laughing because you think something's funny. "That's because I never said anything."

"Why not?"

"I didn't want to be pushy. We'd been friends forever, you know? I figured if he were interested in me, he'd get around to saying something. We were run off our feet that summer, remember? We were spending all our time building the gallery, getting ready to open. I figured if it was meant to be, it would happen."

"Then Johnny met Taylor."

My shoulders sagged. "And that was the end of that."

"And now she's gone after Frank."

"Taylor's not like that, Mel. He must have gone after her."

"She should have tossed him back. For heaven's sake, Cara! She did this to you in college too?"

"It's not her fault that men go for her."

"Why are you defending her?"

"Because how can I blame her if men would rather be with her than me." I tried to stop myself, but the words had been dammed up so long they poured out. "She's funny and flirty and drop-dead gorgeous. Everything I'm not."

"Cara!"

"Don't say it, Mel. I know it's not true."

"Caribou King, stop this right now."

I wanted to stop, but I couldn't. There comes a time when you have to speak the truth no matter how painful it is. "Look at me, Mel. Not as my sister. Look at me as

I really am. I'm a tall gangly string bean with beet-red hair and more freckles than stars in the sky. I know you mean well, you and Mom both, always telling me how pretty I am, but I know better and so does every guy I've ever met. One look at Taylor, and the fat lady sings."

Mel looked as though I'd slapped her in the face. "Cara, I mean it. Cut it out. A real friend wouldn't have slept with Frank knowing you were interested in him."

"Taylor warned me you can't keep a guy waiting, or he'll go somewhere else."

"I don't care what Taylor said. She was out of line."

"It was the first anniversary of Johnny's death. She was hurting so bad, missing him, she didn't know what she was doing."

"That doesn't excuse her."

"Well, what do you want me to do? Whether she should or shouldn't have slept with him, if Frank were really interested in me, he wouldn't have slept with her."

Mel sighed. She walked over to me and put her arms around me. "I'm sorry. You don't need me piling on."

"It's all right. You're not saying anything I haven't thought."

"Someday you're going to find a guy who appreciates all the amazing things you are."

I leaned my head against her shoulder. "You think so?"

"I know so. And don't be so mean to my little sister. She's beautiful whether she knows it or not."

"Maybe I'm doing it wrong. Tay sees what she wants and goes after it until she gets it."

"She goes after men, but what good has it done her?"

I looked at her and made a face, "You really do sound like Mom."

"Stop making excuses for Taylor. She shouldn't have slept with Frank, and you know it."

"It's a moot point now." I shuddered. "Nobody deserves to die like that."

"Maybe it wasn't Frank," said Mel, not very convincingly.

"You said it yourself. If it wasn't Frank, he'd be here."

Kenny knocked just as I was smoothing the last label on the last box. I unlocked the door and led him to the back room. He was sporting his end-of-the-season ball cap this morning, with *Almost Huntin'* emblazoned across a cartoon hunter stalking a worried-looking moose. Stacking boxes on his dolly, I asked if he'd seen Frank yesterday.

"Nah, I heard about it though. Nasty business, that."

"Sure is. I was hoping you'd seen him when he dropped Taylor off at the gallery."

"He dropped her off here?"

"That's what she says. Why?"

"I saw her walkin' along the pier yesterday, but there weren't nobody with her."

"Are you sure it was yesterday?"

Kenny stopped stacking boxes and tilted the dolly back, steadying them as the dolly rocked under the weight. "Thought it was. Days kinda blend together, you know?"

"I hear you. Since we started taking cruise ships, the only day that stands out during the season is Thursday. The others are one big blur."

Kenny laughed. "Light day. You usually have three or four more loads."

After he left, I sat in my office, staring blankly at my computer screen. I looked up at the ceiling, picturing Taylor sleeping in the bedroom above me. Since there were no answers written on the ceiling, I got up and walked into the gallery. "There has to be a logical explanation," I said aloud, trying to drive away the fear that was creeping over me. As usual I found myself in front of Johnny's paintings. No matter what Dan thought, Taylor couldn't have killed Johnny. She was at the gallery when he died.

She could have had an accomplice. The words crossed my thoughts unbidden. Had someone followed Johnny into the woods and murdered him while Taylor was establishing an alibi? Men did things for Taylor, maybe one killed for her. But how do you kill someone and pass it off as a bear attack? The coroner would have seen through that.

Assuming Taylor killed Frank, why would she have wanted him dead? He had followed her out of Mel's, and that was the last I'd seen of him. It was the last anyone admitted to seeing him except for Taylor. Taylor said they'd gone to Frank's place and had been in bed together during the frantic search. I didn't know much about making love to a man, but wouldn't a policeman pounding on the door put a damper on the mood? I could see why you wouldn't want to get up and go to the door, but why not just shout out to him and let him know you were there? Unless you didn't want anyone to know you were there.

Why had Taylor insisted on searching the boat first? Taylor said Frank told her he'd be going home after his tours so that would have been the logical place to look. Only he hadn't finished his tours; he hadn't even started them. He'd gone missing, but Taylor hadn't known that when she searched the boat so why would she have gone there first? Was she alone on the pier yesterday morning, or had Kenny got his days mixed up? No one had been with her when I let her in, and it seemed odd that Frank would have left before Taylor was safely inside. Had the man who'd followed Taylor at the cannery been in the shadows again, and had Frank, confronting him, been killed?

My thoughts returned to the question I'd been asking since the day she'd walked into the gallery. What brought Taylor back to Coho Bay? She'd said she had no other place to go, but with her fortune, she could live anywhere. There was nothing but sadness for her here. True, her home on the island was breathtaking, but there were other beautiful places in the world, all of them less isolated, and none of them as steeped in memory as this one.

Taylor couldn't have killed Johnny. I knew it in my bones. She had come back because this was where they had been happy together, and she hoped it would bring back a little of that happiness. I leaned on the wall, filling the empty spot between the two paintings. She came back because she loved him and wanted nothing more than to be where he had been. Now Dan was accusing her of killing both him and the man with whom she'd sought solace on the anniversary of his death. Reaching out, I put my hand on the nearest frame and felt a charge run though me. "You loved her, Johnny." I whispered. "Show me what to do."

I spent the rest of the day at Mel's. Dan ate his usual eggs and sausage breakfast in record time and asked me to fill his aluminum thermos before he left. "You're in a hurry," I noted, handing back the thermos.

"Gotta meet the state boat. They left Juneau first light, should be here before long."

He left. Not twenty minutes later, a ten-year-old boy, whose father worked at the cannery, poked his head in the door. "Boat's here! They're gonna take the body outta the cannery!"

The restaurant cleared, patrons tossing money on the tables and knocking over chairs in their haste. It might seem ghoulish, but I understood. Frank had been an outsider. He'd kept to himself last winter and worked alone on his boat, spending his off-hours flirting with me more than socializing with the locals. While nobody had anything against him, most people had only a vague idea of who he was, so his murder had none of the pathos that had surrounded Johnny's death and his silent journey to the state police boat. There was only curiosity, and nobody wanted to miss a beat.

Business was so slow with many of the locals spending the day off packing up to leave at the end of the season that when I'd arrived to work the dining room, Bent had been able to persuade Mel to go back to bed. She came down as I finished clearing the dining room, looking refreshed and more relaxed than I'd seen her in a week. "Now I know why they say pregnant women glow," I told her, giving her a hug as she tried to tie on her apron. "You look positively radiant, Mel."

She blushed and pushed me away. "Let me get my apron on so I can help."

"Help with what?" I asked, gesturing toward the empty dining room.

"Where is everybody?" she asked, looking up at the clock.

"Out at the cannery, watching the state police."

The light went out of Mel's face, and she leaned on the counter. "Any news?"

"Not a word."

"Anybody missing besides Frank?"

"Not that I know of."

The chime sounded, and Taylor pushed through the door. She wore a heavy sweater and no coat, so it must've warmed up when the sun came out. Her rich, golden hair was pulled back and knotted at the back her head, and she wore no makeup, and her face looked pale and tired. I couldn't remember the last time I'd seen Taylor without makeup, even in those horrible days after Johnny died.

"Good morning, sleepyhead," I greeted her. "Or should I say good afternoon?"

Taylor climbed up on her regular barstool and looked around the room. "Everybody still in church?"

Mel and I exchanged looks, and I decided it was better not to be honest. "Must be. You want breakfast or lunch?"

"Just coffee."

I poured her a cup and placed it on the counter in front of her, moving cream and sugar into easy reach. "You have to eat, Tay. Bent makes a great egg-white omelet. Add spinach and Swiss cheese, and you'll think you've died and gone to heaven."

Taylor flinched at my unfortunate word choice, but she nodded. I started to head to the kitchen, but Mel stopped me. "I'll go. You sit down, and I'll bring you some lunch. You're probably half-starved by now."

"Thanks, Mel. You think Bent has any moose loaf left?"

She smiled and shook her head as she left. "You'll have to settle for leftover roast beef."

I filled a glass with diet pop and climbed up next to Taylor. "Thanks for the comforter. I must've been more tired than I realized."

"I tried to wake you, but you were out like a light."

"Long day. How are you doing?"

"I've been better."

"Kenny brought the filter back from Juneau. Dad'll be back Wednesday. It'll take him and Bent maybe three or four hours to get it switched out and do a test run, then we can head out to the island. Won't take long to get you moved in and Mr. Peterson moved out."

She sat staring into her coffee cup. "I appreciate your taking care of the place for me, Cara."

"It's a beautiful house, easy to maintain and even easier to rent. I could have rented it four times over, but I chose Mr. Peterson because I knew you wouldn't want a bunch of strangers running in and out of there."

She smiled, more to herself than to me. "You know me too well."

"I feel the same way about renting out my place while I'm out at the folk's place every winter."

"You let Frank live there last year?"

"He needed a place, and the renter I'd had in there the year before decided to go stateside."

"You're going to stay in town this year, aren't you?"

"Probably. Only question will be whether Mom and Dad stay at my place and I stay here or the other way around."

Taylor laughed. "Your mother isn't going to let you live alone, and she isn't going to let your Dad take her three blocks away from that baby."

"Well, she'll have to pick one or the other because we can't all stay here. Although maybe the three of us should stay here and let Mel and Bent live at my place. It's the only way they'll be getting any privacy this winter."

"Privacy is overrated." Mel beamed as she put the plates in front of us. I pulled the top off my sandwich and frowned. "Horseradish sauce. I forgot you actually like that stuff. Let me go get it."

I slid off my stool. "I'll get it. Why don't you get something to eat and join us? Bent too. We'll even sit at a table."

"That'd be fun," Taylor chimed in. Her voice was not as cheerful as her words, but at least she was trying, so Mel left to get Bent.

"Come on, Tay," I said, grabbing the horseradish sauce from behind the counter and picking up my plate. "Let's take a table by the window."

Taylor picked up her plate and her coffee and followed me. I claimed the window seat, and she took the aisle. "I'll go get my pop, and I'll grab you a pot for when you want refills."

"And my sugar, please. There isn't any over here."

I managed all three over in one trip. "That's because nobody but you puts fake sugar in their coffee."

"And nobody but you calls 'soda' pop," she said, a little of her humor returning.

I enjoyed her lighthearted mood even if I knew it would be fleeting. "Six of one, half dozen of the other."

Mel and Bent came out of the kitchen to find us both giggling. "What are you two so giddy about?" asked Mel. She put down their drinks, juice for both of them, and sat across from me. Bent put Mel's salad in front of her and sat down across from Taylor. He had the biggest bacon cheeseburger I'd ever seen, complete with a batch of his homemade chips.

"Hey, how come you didn't make me any chips?" I said, eyeing his. "All I have is coleslaw."

"You like coleslaw," said Mel, "and it's better for you."

I rolled my eyes, and Bent transferred a handful of chips to my plate without significantly denting the mountain on his own. "Knew you'd want some, so I made extra," he said, winking at me while Mel poked him in the arm. "Taylor?"

"No thanks, but you do make a mean egg-white omelet."

"Not much demand for them when there's no cruise ship in town. Locals are more the extra meat, heavy on the cheese sauce type."

"Nothing wrong with a little cheese sauce," I said.

"I don't know where you put it," said Taylor, perhaps with a hint of envy. She turned to Mel. "Are you having a boy or a girl?"

"We don't want to know," said Mel, "We want to find out the old-fashioned way."

"I'll help you paint the guest room green," I offered, and Mel kicked me.

"Mom and Dad might not like you painting the room with them in it! Besides, we'll have plenty of time to paint the room pink or blue after the baby's born."

"There's no way Mom's going to be happy living five miles into the woods once that baby comes, Mel. You'd better think about building an addition."

"Don't even joke about it, Cara," warned Bent. He looked at Mel. "She is joking, right?"

Without taking her eyes off her husband, Mel kicked me again, this time far more painfully. "Of course she is, honey."

"Why don't you let your folks have your apartment after the baby comes, Cara? You can stay with me. I'm sure I'll be ready for company by then."

"Thanks, Taylor," said Mel. "I don't want to sound selfish, but I don't like the idea of Cara being so far away after the baby comes."

"Then stop kicking me."

"Who's kicking you? Your leg just keeps getting in the way of my foot."

"Ladies," said Bent, and we subsided.

"It's not that far away," Taylor persisted. "She can come into town whenever she wants."

"Doesn't the water around the island freeze?" asked Mel.

"Nah, Johnny had it dredged when he moved out there," answered Bent. "He didn't want to have to keep pulling his boat out of the water."

"I know we kept the boat in the water all winter," agreed Taylor, "but I never thought much about it. How could Johnny have afforded to have dredging done? Isn't that horribly expensive?"

"I don't rightly know," admitted Bent. "Maybe he bartered for it. We do a lot of that around here."

"True."

"Except you don't have a boat," I said.

"I forgot. Jack took Johnny's boat after he died. He said they'd bought it together, so it seemed only fair for him to have it."

Bent snorted. "Jack didn't buy that boat."

"What do you mean?"

"Johnny bought it with money he inherited from his mom. She left him the house too. It'd been in her family for generations."

"Johnny never told me his mother grew up here."

"She didn't," I said, letting Bent get back to his lunch. "It was a vacation home. Her family has been coming here off and on since before I was born. That's why she and Jack chose Coho Bay when they decided to live in Alaska full time."

"Why didn't they live on the island?"

"They did for a while, at least in the winters. They lived at the mill in the summer. Once Johnny was old enough to go to school, they moved into town like my folks did."

"And you and Johnny grew up together? That's what he always said."

"You might be able to take Dad's boat," offered Mel, saving me from what was becoming an uncomfortable conversation.

"I wouldn't say this around your dad," said Bent, "since I know how proud he is of that boat, but that thing's held together with duct tape and baling wire. I wouldn't want to have you all the way out there, relying on a boat that breaks down every time you look at it cross-eyed. Look how fast that filter went bad."

"That's a good point," agreed Mel. "Now that you mention it, we shouldn't just take Taylor out there and dump her on the island with no way off."

"I'll be fine," said Taylor.

"There's Frank's boat," said Bent, stopping the conversation in its tracks. "It was just a thought. Maybe you could rent it."

"From who?" I asked. "Anybody hear Frank talk about his family?" Three heads shook.

"Wouldn't he have listed an emergency contact on his rental application?" asked Taylor. Eyes rolled, giving her an answer. We didn't go in for that kind of formality here.

"Dan'll track down the next of kin," said Bent. "Whoever they are, I can't imagine they'll need it before spring. I'm sure they'd rent it to you, Taylor."

"I don't think Taylor should express any interest in that boat," said Mel quietly.

We let her words soak in, forced to remember that in Dan's eyes, Taylor was a suspect. I broke the silence. "Maybe you should rent it, Bent, and just let Tay use it when you don't need it. Hey, I wonder if we could convince Dad to buy it if it comes on the market."

"You're being morbid, don't you think?" asked Mel.

"She has a point, hon, we need a better boat. I don't have any money, and I don't think your dad can afford to buy it right now, but maybe we could do a rental."

"I could go in on it with you guys. Maybe all together we could swing it."

"Will you guys stop talking about Frank like he's dead? It's positively ghoulish how you're already dividing up his things." All eyes turned to Taylor. There were patches of red on her cheeks, and her eyes blazed.

I felt horribly guilty. "I'm sorry, Tay."

"Of course you're right, Taylor. Let's pray that Frank is alive and well and will walk through that door laughing at all of us for having ever thought otherwise." Just then the door chimed, and we all turned to stare at it, wondering if Mel's words had gone straight to God's ears, but it was only Dan. Four groans of disappointment greeted him.

"Nice to see you too," he said.

"I'm sorry, Dan," said Bent, getting up. "Can I get you anything?"

"One of those would be great," said Dan, pointing at what was left of Bent's burger. "Where you been hiding them?"

"I'd have to charge twice as much to put burgers like these on the menu, but I'll see what I can do for you. Have a seat."

Bent picked up his plate and empty juice glass and gestured for Dan to take his place. Mel started to get up, but Bent told her to finish her lunch. Dan sat down and looked around the table. We must have looked guilty. "Why are you all looking at me like that? Whole town's talking about the murder. No reason why you shouldn't."

"Did the state police have any answers?" I asked, thankful we didn't have to tell him what we'd really been talking about.

"Nah, just took the body and some things from the cabin and the boat they thought would have DNA on them."

"Did they find blood on the boat? Do they think that's where… it… happened?"

"Cara, I can't talk about what they may or may not have found."

"Did they take the boat with them?" I jumped when Mel kicked my leg.

"Why would they do that?"

I felt the heat rise to my face. I was really going to have to learn how to control that reaction. "Just asking."

"Well, just stop asking questions you know I can't answer." He pulled a key from his pocket and handed it to Mel. "Thanks for the loan."

"Does this mean we can rent out the cabin again now?" I asked. "Stop kicking me, Mel!"

"Get a lot of demand for dry cabins in the off-season, do you?" Dan thanked Bent, who had made him a burger not quite as big as his own but bigger than usual. Bent held his hand out to Mel as customers had started trickling in.

"Don't you worry, Mel. I've got it," I said, getting up and motioning for her to sit.

"Stop treating me like a hothouse flower. Let me work until I'm so big I don't want to do anything. Besides, don't you have a renter leaving today?"

"Oh shoot! I completely forgot. I'd better get out to the cabins, or he'll leave without me."

"Want me to come with you?" asked Taylor.

"No need. I can check out renters in my sleep."

"Can I borrow your key? I locked the apartment when I left."

I pulled the key off my ring and handed it to her. "Why don't you stop by Longman's and have one made? That way you won't have to keep asking me." Longman's General Store sat a block off the main drag. They stocked groceries and basic supplies, and they had the only key grinder in town.

"I'll do that, thanks. I'll leave yours with Mel so if I go for a walk you won't be stuck."

"Thanks, Tay." I said good-bye to Dan and shrugged into my coat for the mile walk to the cabins. It was warm enough that by the time I got there I happily shed the coat as I knocked on the door.

"Morning, Cara. Wondered if you forgot about me. I'm all ready to go."

"I'm sorry. I would have been here earlier, but it's been a bit crazy around town lately."

He stepped out of the cabin, carrying one bag and hoisting a large backpack onto his shoulder. He handed me his key. "I noticed all the police activity." He nodded at Frank's cabin, two cabins away from his. "What's up?"

"Frank Baker is missing."

He dropped his backpack and stared at me. "No fooling? I'm sorry to hear that. He seemed like a nice guy. I hope he's okay. After that poor guy got killed last year, I've been carrying bear spray."

"Me too." I was glad he hadn't heard about the body hauled out of the bay. "Did you see much of Frank?"

He leaned against the porch railing and stared thoughtfully at the other cabin. "Just to say hello and good-bye. Couple of nights ago, I guess, was the last time I saw him. You were over there last night, weren't you? Pounding on the door?"

"Yes, sorry we made so much noise. We were worried about him."

"Then I saw him the night before that."

I felt my heartbeat pick up speed. "Friday night?"

He nodded. "He came home late. He was always quiet. I wouldn't have heard him except I'd had a little too much of that chili your brother-in-law makes. It's good stuff, but oh, man-a-mighty, fella can't sleep after that."

"You happen to notice what time it was?"

"Round about two in the morning. I remember thinkin' it wasn't like him to be comin' home so late."

"Was he alone?"

"Sure. Never saw him bring anyone home with him. 'Cept the policeman. He came over a few times. Seemed to be friendly visits, nothin' to worry about."

My heart was pounding so strongly I had to sit back on the porch railing so I wouldn't fall down. He hadn't seen Taylor, who'd claimed she was with Frank all night. Frank had gone into the cabin at two, but Taylor had said they'd been in the cabin when Dan checked it before midnight. What had Dan been doing visiting Frank? I hadn't even known they knew each other except in passing.

My renter didn't seem to notice my distress. He bid me a cheerful farewell, and I plastered on a smile that faded the moment his back was turned. I listened to his whistle fade and willed myself to calm down. There must be a reasonable answer. Maybe Taylor had been with Frank at midnight and he'd walked her back to town, well, after. Finding the apartment still locked, maybe he settled her in his boat and went home, which would account for Kenny seeing her alone early in the morning.

What kind of man would have sex with a woman then bundle her off a mile down the road, then leave her alone on a boat in the freezing cold predawn and walk another mile back to a dry cabin? Somebody was lying. I couldn't think of any reason why my renter would lie, which could only mean that Taylor was lying about where she and Frank had been that night. Why would she lie about that, knowing that Frank could easily discredit her?

My head ached, and I rubbed my temples, trying to soothe away the pain. No, no, no, no, no! Taylor could not possibly have known that Frank had been beyond the ability to discredit anyone. There had to be another explanation. I forced myself away from the railing. I needed to get the cabin ready for winter. There was no plumbing to winterize, so I cleaned out the wood stove, dumping the ashes in the metal container made for that purpose. I stacked firewood next to the hearth in case some hiker or hunter got caught in a storm this winter and needed to use the cabin for shelter. Dad always had me leave two of the cabins unlocked with a special symbol on the door. When I opened the cabins in the spring, I often found thank-you notes.

Finished, I walked over to Frank's cabin and checked the door. It was locked. I peeked in the window, but the curtain was still drawn. I wished I'd thought to bring my passkey with me, but it was hanging on a hook in my apartment. "What happened to you, Frank?" I whispered, leaning on the door. For a moment I pictured it opening, spilling me on the floor and making me laugh up into the face of a very much alive and amused Frank Baker. The door stayed solidly closed, and the cabin beyond was silent. I thought of the headless body and shuddered. "Please don't let that be you."

Chapter 9

I walked slowly back into town, my thoughts racing, the spectacular view wasted on me. The bells tied into my shoelaces made a cheerful noise that my heart didn't echo. No one was quite sure how effective bells were as bear deterrents, but I usually enjoyed the happy sound enough to wear them anyway. My father delights in telling tourists you can identify bear scat by the presence of bells, and sometimes they believe him until they catch sight of the twinkle in his eye. Like whistling past a graveyard, it may not help, but it certainly didn't hurt, so most people wore bells in spring and fall. Today the bells only made me sad.

I noticed the state police boat pulling away from the cannery on its way back to Juneau. The thought of what it carried robbed the air from my lungs, and I sat down unceremoniously on the dirt road. It didn't matter that Frank had slept with Taylor. He had been my friend, a smile I'd depended on all season long. He'd stepped up to protect Taylor when Jack had threatened her at Mel's. Now he was nothing more than a mutilated body on a ship bound for the state capital.

The sun offered me no warmth as I sat there, rocked by the sudden and brutal fate that had befallen the man whose eyes had danced with mischief whenever he looked at me. My thoughts inevitably turned to Johnny, who'd met his own fate just as suddenly. I pulled my knees up to my chin and locked my arms around my legs and shook. How long I sat there I couldn't say, but when I looked up, the boat was gone and the wind was blowing clouds over the sun, stealing the light and warning me I'd better get moving or risk being caught outside when the storm hit.

I scrambled to my feet and started walking. I took a shortcut across lots when I got to the outskirts of town and headed for my apartment. Reaching the alley behind the gallery, I stopped short and ducked back behind the fence I'd just rounded. Taylor was standing in the alley, engaged in whispered conversation with a man. His back was to me so I couldn't see who he was, but her face bore a harsh and angry look I'd never seen before. I was too far away to hear what they were saying, but her words and her gestures spoke volumes.

She was clearly upset and making that point undeniably clear to her companion, who couldn't have been saying much judging from the fact that Taylor was doing all the talking. The man finally put his hands on her shoulders and leaned his head down, saying something that seemed to soothe her because her body relaxed slightly and her face lost some of its edge. I pulled back and leaned against the fence, confused at what I'd seen. Taylor didn't know anyone in Coho Bay, certainly no one she would know well enough for what had felt like such an intimate moment.

By the time I had the good sense to peek around the fence again, they were both gone. I kicked the fence in frustration. I'd missed the chance to see the man's face or at least the direction he'd gone. The apartment forgotten, I turned and marched straight to Mel's, pushing the doors open and letting them crash behind me. I stomped through the empty dining room and pushed open the kitchen door. This time it was Mel and Bent whose intimate moment I interrupted, though I was too upset to recognize that I was intruding and walk away.

"What's happened?" asked Mel. "Cara, you look like you've seen a ghost."

I dug up a smile though it seemed to do little to reassure her. "Nothing. Everything. I don't know, Mel."

"You're white as a sheet. What is it?"

"I have to sit down." I pulled a stool out from under the worktable and sat down hard. Mel sat more gracefully beside me and waited. In halting fashion, trying to take hold of my own jumbled emotions as I talked, I told them what the renter had said about Frank.

"Which means Taylor lied about being with Frank," said Mel. "Why would she do that?"

"And where was she since she wasn't at the cabin? Kenny said he's sure he saw her walking alone on the pier the next morning. What would she be doing out there?"

"I don't know, Cara."

"But that isn't all. I was cutting through the alley on the way home and caught Taylor with some guy behind the gallery."

"Doing what?" asked Mel.

"Throwing a fit. I was too far away to hear what she was saying, but she wasn't letting him get a word in. Then he put his hands on her shoulders and whispered something, and she seemed to calm down."

"Who was he?" asked Bent.

"I have no idea. I only saw him from the back. Who does she know well enough to have that kind of conversation with?" I looked from one face to the other, but puzzled expressions were all I saw.

"Wait!" said Mel. "Could it have been Frank?"

"Do you think?" Then I shook my head. "I don't think so."

"Are you sure?"

"Pretty sure. He wasn't tall enough to have been Frank."

"Didn't he look at all familiar?"

"No, Mel, his back didn't remind me of anyone. And don't ask about his hair. He had a hat on. One of those knitted ones that only everybody wears."

"What about his coat?" asked Bent.

I closed my eyes. "Cloth, tan, probably lined from the bulk."

"Like the one Dan wears."

I opened my eyes and looked hard at Bent. "Dan thinks Tay's a black widow. Why would he be huddled with her behind the gallery?"

"I didn't say it was Dan, just that he has a coat like that."

"Lots of guys have coats like that."

"Is he the right height?" asked Mel.

"It wasn't Dan," I insisted.

The back door opened, and we all turned to look. It was Taylor, so our conversation abruptly shifted. "Hey, Tay. I was just going over to check on you."

"I'm fine. Everybody can stop worrying about me." She walked over to the pot that was simmering on the stove and sniffed. "That smells good. Gumbo?"

"Alaskan Gumbo," said Bent with the smile of any cook who loves compliments about his food.

"You're a magician, you know. What you do with leftovers is amazing."

"Thanks." Bent was not quite succeeding in keeping the pride out of his voice. "I figure no reason to be boring just because we're on the edge of nowhere."

"We're not nowhere," said Mel. "We're smack-dab in the middle of where we belong."

"Speaking of where we belong, have you decided where everyone is sleeping this winter?" I said, reverting to a safe topic.

"They're building a house in the vacant lot behind the restaurant," said Taylor.

"What? Who told you that?" asked Mel, looking a little panicked.

"You wait and see," said Tay, smiling.

"I'm betting they're going to start construction the minute they get the news," I added, glancing obviously at Mel's belly.

"That'd be a sucker bet knowing your folks," said Bent. "At least they'll be in one house and we'll be in the other.

"Unless they tear down the back wall and just build an extension here," I said, stifling a giggle.

"Stop laughing, Cara. If they do build back there, you know they'll put in a room for you."

That was a sobering thought, so I stopped teasing Mel. Instead, I asked about the baby, and that diverted her attention away from me for the better part of an hour. I stole looks at Taylor as we talked, examining her for any hint of the scene I'd witnessed. She seemed relaxed and comfortable, perhaps a little sad around the eyes, but she seemed happy for Mel and Bent as they talked about their plans.

She acted no different than the Taylor I'd always known, yet there was something in her words and her movements that bothered me. I wasn't sure whether it was because there was something new, or whether it had always been there, but I was only beginning to see. Either way it was disquieting. The end of the season couldn't come soon enough. I'd take her out to the island, pick up Mr. Peterson, and put all the uncertainty behind me. Surely some time to let the dust settle could only do our friendship good.

And yet I knew it wasn't going to be that simple. A body had been pulled from the bay, and regardless of his identity, the one thing I knew for certain was that the poor man's death hadn't been accidental. Somewhere in Coho Bay was a killer who might be poised to strike again. Until Dan had him under lock and key, no one was safe. Much as I was ready to put a little distance between us, it wasn't safe for Taylor to be living by herself on the island right now.

"Cara?"

I had lost track of the conversation, and I hadn't realized it until Mel put her hand on my arm and squeezed. I blinked my eyes and focused on her. "I'm sorry. Were you talking to me?"

"Sheesh, Cara," said Taylor, her voice grating on me in a way it hadn't before. "You're a million miles away."

"We were talking about where everyone is gonna live this winter," explained Mel. "Taylor and Bent think it might be best for you to stay on the island. That way Taylor won't be out there all alone."

"No!" The word shot out before I could stop it. Taylor's crestfallen look gave me a twinge of regret, but I ruthlessly ignored it. "I don't want to be so far away from you, Mel."

That made Mel happy, but it didn't convince Bent. "Why? You'll only be a boat ride away."

"We don't have a boat, remember? We talked about that this morning."

"If you'd been paying attention," said Taylor, "you'd know we have a solution for that."

"Cady McMartin stopped by today. He's gonna be working the oil fields up north and wanted to know if I'd look after his boat," said Bent.

Cady was a local fisherman. He had gotten a job in Prudhoe Bay where he would spend the winter looking after oil field equipment. The conditions were harsh, but the pay was good, and by the time Cady would be itching to get his boat in the water next spring, the field workers would be back for the drilling season. He had a boat twice as big as Dad's, which he kept in tip-top shape as did all the men whose livelihoods depended on the sea.

I shot Mel a desperate look, and she came through like a trooper. "Which means that Taylor won't be isolated. You can run out for her anytime she wants to come into town, so Cara can stay here. I'd really prefer to have her here with me. Pregnant woman's prerogative."

"I can't argue with that," said Bent, picking up on the change in mood if he wasn't quite sure what had caused it.

"I understand," said Taylor.

I could tell she'd picked up on the mood shift and was hurt by it, but I bit my tongue to keep from giving in to her. I didn't think she was a murderer, but I was seeing her in a new light and the thought of being cooped up on the island with her all winter was more than I could bear.

"Just give me a buzz on the shortwave, Taylor," said Bent, still looking a bit confused.

"Oh, I'll be fine, Bent. Don't give it a second thought."

That would have worked on me yesterday, but in my simmering annoyance I heard a manipulative tone in her that I hadn't noticed before. If we kept traveling down this road, it would ruin our friendship. Time and distance, that's what we needed. Her feelings might be hurt now, but it would be worth it once I'd had a chance to recover my equilibrium. I decided to change topics. "What's this about Jack lying to Taylor about Johnny's boat? I've half a mind to go out there and give him a piece of my mind."

"Let it go, Cara," said Taylor. "I was pretty sure he was lying at the time, but I didn't care. If it makes Jack happy to have the boat, let him have it."

"You know," said Mel, "I don't think I've ever seen Jack take the boat out, but I'm always here." She gestured around the kitchen. "He could take out a fleet of boats and it would be news to me."

"I don't know what he did with the boat, now that you mention it." Bent rubbed the stubble on his chin. "I don't know that I've noticed it in the marina, but then I'm usually here too." He ran a finger along her cheek, and Taylor and I were suddenly in the way.

"Let's go look, Tay," I said, pushing her out the door in front of me. Looking back at them, I don't think Mel and Bent even realized we were leaving.

"Why do I care what Jack did with the boat?" grumbled Taylor when I'd closed the door.

"You don't. I just thought they would appreciate a little privacy." The day had turned cold, and I pulled up the hood on my coat and buried my hands in my pockets. "I hope the snow holds off."

"It doesn't usually snow until November. Johnny told me that."

I laughed, a little of my wariness fading. "We tell everybody that when we're trying to get them to stay. Remember that first storm?"

"October 3. Johnny said it was a fluke."

"An annual one." I was being a little hard on her, but snow was part of life in Alaska. The panhandle, as people called this land along the Inland Passage, has a milder climate than the interior of the state because we have the warmth of the sea currents that cities like Fairbanks lacked. Winter came in fits and spurts here. Some days were beautiful and warm, others brought sudden rain or snow squalls. It could be ten degrees one day and forty the next, then just as easily the temperatures could plummet below zero. It was why the ships deserted us October through April.

We reached the marina in record time, the cold inspiring a brisk pace. There were no assigned slips in Coho Bay. Locals and guests parked at whatever slip was available. Being creatures of habit, as they did with the seating at Mel's, everyone parked pretty close to where they always did. "Where did Johnny tie up?"

"As close to town as we could get," answered Taylor. "We usually came in when Johnny had paintings to deliver. He didn't like to walk too far with them."

We went out one side of the dock and back the other, looking at each boat. We didn't find Johnny's among them. We walked a little further and went out and back the shorter second arm, but we still didn't find the boat. "Could Jack have sold it?" I asked Taylor.

"Not legally since the estate hasn't settled. He might be letting someone else use it. It's the same with the island. I have use of it, but I couldn't sell it."

"Taylor, why hasn't the estate settled?"

"Let's go look along the commercial side."

"No, we're not going to look along the commercial side." I sat down on a bench. "Taylor, I've asked a lot of questions since you came back, and I'm tired of you not giving me any answers. I'm not taking another step until you start talking."

Taylor took a few steps away from me then stopped, her back to me. "Jack contested the will. He came to court and told the judge there's evidence that I set Johnny up to be killed."

"That's ridiculous. How do you set someone up to be killed by a bear? Why would the judge believe such a crazy story?"

She spun around and spit out the words. "He accused me of having a lover attack Johnny in the woods and leave him for dead. He said I had Johnny take me to the gallery that day so I'd have an alibi. Then Dan

Simmons told the judge Johnny's death was under investigation, so he agreed to put a hold on the estate."

I stammered something out but even I wasn't sure what I was saying. I felt as though my head were the center of a bass drum, and every word pounded until I couldn't think anymore. I finally got my tongue under control. "For how long?"

"How long what?"

"How long is the hold? They can't keep the estate in limbo forever. There must be some kind of evidence."

"There isn't any evidence because I didn't do anything! Don't tell me you think I'd ever hurt Johnny! Is that why you suddenly can't stand to be parted from Mel?"

"She's having a baby."

She threw up her hands and looked up at the darkening clouds. "Isn't it rich? I come back because you're the one person in the whole world I actually trust, and this is what I get? Jack's right. I should just kill myself and be done with it."

My head shot up. "What are you talking about?"

"When I left Mel's that night, I got to the apartment and realized I couldn't get in. I kicked the door a couple of times, and then I started back to the road."

"You told me that before."

"Yes. Only I didn't tell you that Jack was there, standing under the awning across from the gallery."

"Mr. Shoes!" I said, then remembered Jack had been passed out the first time I saw the watcher.

"Maybe. All I know is he went off on me big time. I tried to ignore him, but he wouldn't let me by. He was saying all kinds of ugly things. I was scared he was gonna do something crazy."

"I saw Frank follow you out of the restaurant."

"That's right! He got right in Jack's face and made him back down."

"Jack knew Frank could kick the crap out of him."
At least, I thought he could have. Jack was older, but he
was strong from years of working in the mill. He might
have given Frank a run for his money if he hadn't been
drunk, which these days he nearly always was when he
wasn't working.

"Frank tossed me his keys and told me to wait for
him in the boat, so I did."

"So Frank took Jack home then came back for you?"

She looked away from me. "That's what I assumed
he was going to do."

"You assumed? Why don't you know?"

She looked back at me, and there were tears running
down her face. Taylor was not allergic to mascara, and
the effect would have been comical if the subject
weren't so serious. "Cara, he never came."

As the impact of her words sunk in, I felt as though
I'd been punched in the gut. "What? But you said—"

"I know what I said. You asked where I'd been, and
I just—"

"Lied. You lied to me. A lie you knew would hurt
me."

"I wasn't thinking." She sat down on the bench
beside me and took my hand. "I'm sorry."

I pulled my hand away and stood up. "Of course you
were thinking. You were thinking of the only person
you ever think of, and it wasn't me. You said the first
thing that popped into your head, and you've been lying
about it ever since. You even lied to the police during a
murder investigation. Have you lost your mind?"

"Cara—"

"No! Whatever you have to say, I don't want to hear
it. I've heard enough of your lies for any one lifetime,
and I don't want to hear any more." I started to walk
away, then I stopped. "Get your things and get out of
my apartment. You can stay at the cabins. I'll pick up

Mr. Peterson as soon as Dad gets the boat running, and then you can get someone to run you out there. Live there or don't. I'm out."

"I don't have anywhere to go, and even if I did, I don't have any money to get there. I spent every dime I had to get here." Taylor's voice, small and sad and quiet, cut through me.

I didn't turn around because I didn't want to let her work on me. "What do you mean you have no money? What about the fortune you inherited from your parents? Was that a lie too?"

"I never said they left me a fortune. That was your assumption."

"If it was, you didn't set me straight."

"Because it didn't matter. You liked me for me, not for the money you thought I had. Johnny did too. He knew exactly how much money I had, and he didn't care. We had plenty, and that was all that mattered."

"You spent every penny?"

"We combined our money after we got married, and when he died I couldn't get a dime, not even what I'd put in. All I had was Johnny's life insurance."

"Which left you with nothing to live on in Seattle."

"So I came here. I knew I could live on the island until the estate settled."

I turned to face her. I hated to admit it, but there wasn't a false note in her story. If she was lying, I couldn't tell. "How long can they tie up the estate?"

"I only have to make it through another month."

"Without them arresting you."

"I didn't do anything. Cara, you've got to believe me."

I wanted to believe her. I was almost there, then I remembered she'd said Jack accused her of having a lover, and I thought of the stranger I'd seen her with. "Who was the man you were with behind the gallery today?" Her face went positively white, and the last thin thread of hope I'd been holding on to broke. "Yeah, you let me know when you've thought up a lie to explain him."

I spun around and walked away, half expecting her to follow but glad she didn't. I didn't feel like going back to the apartment, and I didn't want to explain myself to Mel, so I turned right instead of left. I walked to the end of the harbor road, then turned up the street that ran along the far side of the bay. I didn't get out here often. It was residential, and I preferred woodlands to houses, but there was a pleasant pathway that ran along the water's edge, and I left the sidewalk to follow it. I walked slowly, trying to put my thoughts in order. I passed the last house and kept walking until I reached a rocky outcrop overlooking the bay. I left the path and scrambled up the rocks, finding a spot tucked out of the wind, just above the high-water mark.

From here I had a good view of Johnny's island. It was about a hundred yards off shore, just inside the mouth of the bay. The waning sun had caught one of the windows, and it glinted golden from the cover of the trees. It was a small island, heavily wooded. I knew there were paths through the woods that Johnny had kept clear of brush so he and Taylor could walk together. Johnny had installed a metal dock with a covered boathouse and a lift so he could take his boat out of the water during bad storms.

It would have been expensive to replace the old wooden dock with a metal one and to build the boathouse with its lift. Dredging the slip would have added to the total. Where had Johnny come by that much money? I'd assumed that it had been Taylor's money when Bent mentioned it, but if I could believe her, she hadn't had that kind of money. I knew Johnny's mother left him some money when she'd died.

He'd told me that it was enough to enable him to paint full time but that it was his dream to someday support himself as a painter. That hadn't sounded like a man with a substantial bank balance.

Jack had accused Taylor of being a gold digger. I'd dismissed it because I'd thought the money had been hers, but now I wasn't sure. Maybe Johnny's mother had left him more than I'd thought, at least enough money that Jack thought it was worth fighting over. You'd be hard-pressed to guess anybody's net worth in Coho Bay. My own parents were a good example. They'd both come from money, and they both had good jobs. They had spent frugally and invested wisely over the years, allowing them to set Mel and Bent up with the restaurant and me with the gallery, and they'd flatly refused our offers to pay them back. They owned quite a bit of property in and around town, and their income from rentals had ballooned when the cruise ships put Coho Bay on the travel radar. We had seen an influx of summer visitors who didn't come and go in a day but who stayed for a few weeks or even the whole season as Mr. Peterson had.

So Dan had gone to court with Jack and sworn that there was some kind of evidence to support an investigation into Taylor's involvement in Johnny's death. I wondered what it would take to convince a judge but not damning enough for him to be able to arrest her. Was the man behind the gallery Taylor's lover-turned-accomplice? She'd been back less than a week, and that man had not seemed like someone she'd just met. Had they been carrying on an affair and decided to get rid of her husband? Even if they had, you can't kill someone by getting a bear to attack him. Dan had warned me about Taylor, so maybe he knew something I didn't.

I needed to ask him about it. I stood up, then sat back down. Dan already suspected Taylor of being involved in Johnny's death. If I told him about the man, it could be very damaging to her and it wouldn't be fair to implicate her when it might have been an innocent conversation. A man had been murdered though. Maybe two men if Johnny's death was somehow not an accident, and if that were true I had no reason to protect her. If she was telling the truth, she had nothing to fear.

Dan had told me the last person who'd admitted to seeing Frank was Taylor, and according to what she was saying now, she'd last seen him with Jack. My renter had seen Frank come home much later, alone. That fit Taylor's revised version of the night's events, and it made more sense now that she would go to the boat when we set out to look for him. Taylor's new account had the ring of truth that had been missing from her earlier tale, so the next logical step would be for someone to talk to Jack.

I climbed off my perch and headed back into town. At city hall I poked my head into Dan's office. It was empty. "Where'd he go?" I asked Tammy, the senior citizen who greeted visitors.

"Home, I hope. He's been bitin' people's heads off all mornin.'"

"Why?"

"Them state boys musta rattled his chain. Think they know ever'thing up in Juneau."

"If you see him, could you tell him I'm looking for him?"

"Shore thing, hunny. You sweet on Danny?"

"Dan? Tammy, how desperate do you think I am?"

She took the horn-rimmed glasses from her face and let them hang by the chain around her neck. "Now you listen' to me, dearie. It don't pay to be too picky. There ain't nothin' wrong with Danny that a good woman cain't fix."

"I'll keep that in mind. You let him know I need to talk to him, okay?"

"I'll tell him, but you just think about it. There ain't so many men around here that you can keep givin' them away."

"Haven't you heard there are five men for every woman in Alaska?"

She laughed, a high, squeaky snort. "That mighta been true in my day, missy, but it ain't true now, and it shore ain't true in Coho Bay."

She was right, so I quit while I was behind and left, listening to the snort fade as I got further down the street. I pulled out my cell phone and called Dan. I got his voice mail, the bane of modern existence. What good did it do to carry a cell phone if you weren't going to answer it? "Dan, it's Cara. I'm headed out to the mill to talk to Jack. I found out a couple of things that may have something to do with the murder, so I probably ought to tell you about them. Give me a call when you get this."

Considering the mood Jack had been in lately, I thought about checking to see if Bent would go with me when I passed the restaurant, but I decided against it. I still had my handgun in my pocket if I needed to defend myself, but I couldn't imagine I'd need it. Jack might be a bully, but he wasn't a murderer. Bullies back down when you stand up to them, so I wasn't afraid of him. He had been angry with me for introducing Johnny to Taylor, but it was her he hated, not me. I headed out of town, past the cabins and out to the end of the road where Jack's sawmill was located. I hadn't been there in years, not since high school when I used to go out now and then to have dinner with Johnny and his parents. It had been a way to break up the long winters, and I had visited several of the homes of the guys on my football team.

Johnny hadn't ever played football. I think his artist's eye couldn't bear to see the bruises and blood that even our tame brand of play produced. As I'd told Frank, I'd been drafted to round out the team because when Johnny decided not to play, our little school didn't have enough boys to field even a six-man team. I hadn't minded playing, partly because it bothered my mother and partly because what girl wouldn't want to be surrounded by every boy in her class? The downside of playing football was that after graduation I found the only single men my age had become pals and teammates. It's harder than you'd expect for a boy to fall in love with his quarterback, and one by one my former teammates had grown up and married other girls.

I didn't see Jack's truck parked at the mill or by his house, which stood about fifty feet further off the road, under the shelter of the trees. Climbing the steps into the mill, I saw why. *Gone hunting* was written in block letters on cardboard and stuck with a thumbtack into the doorframe. "Crap," I said, kicking the door in my disappointment. I don't know what I'd been planning to say to Jack, but now that I was here, it was frustrating to not be able to say it.

I don't know what possessed me to try the door. I had a vague idea that maybe I'd leave Jack a note and ask him to come see me when he got back, but whatever idea I might have had, it packed its bags and left the moment I opened that door. Of course it wasn't locked. Not everybody in Coho Bay has a paranoid and now missing friend who makes her lock her door, but poor Jack might have been better off if he'd had someone like Frank looking after him.

The smell hit me, then the flies. Then the sickly but unmistakable stench of blood and lots of it, judging by the sheer number of the flies. I didn't set foot inside. I leaned over the deck railing and threw up into the bushes. I was bent over, still reeling, when Dan's truck pulled into the lot, and I can honestly say I was never gladder to see anyone in my entire life. Wiping my mouth with the back of my hand, I stood there rooted to the spot and waited for him to join me on the stoop. I had a fleeting thought that I should walk down to meet him, but my feet wouldn't move and my hands refused to let go of the railing, so I'd stood there, waiting, feeling the world spinning around me.

"What happened to you?" said Dan glibly, but my weakened condition must have impressed itself upon him, and I thought I detected a note of concern.

"Blood. Flies. Everywhere." Not the most intelligent line I'd ever spoken, but I was surprised I could muster even that much, all things considered. Just uttering those three words had brought the memory of that smell back to me, and I leaned over the railing again.

"Stay here," said Dan when I was able to straighten up again. He didn't have to tell me that. There was no way I was going to follow him. I had seen enough to know I didn't want to see anything more. He pulled a handkerchief from his pocket and held it over his nose and mouth. Taking a deep breath, he opened the door and closed it quickly after him, but not so quickly that the smell hadn't come billowing out.

I threw up again. You'd think I'd have a stronger stomach, having been a hunter half my life, but there's a big difference between the fresh kill of a game animal and the who-knows-how-long-ago murder of a human being. I leaned my head against the rail and blessed the metal for being cool against my skin. I fought to stay upright. Dan must have come back out again because I heard the door and, well, you know what I smelled. I closed my eyes and rocked against the railing. My knees began to buckle.

I felt Dan's arm go around my waist. "Come on, Cara. Let's get you away from the door."

"Thank merciful God for you, Dan." I don't know that I've ever thanked God for the appearance of a man before, but at that moment it seemed faint praise. "Is he... dead?"

"Somebody's dead, from all that blood, but there's no body."

He pulled open the truck's passenger door and lifted me into the seat. I tried to climb up, but my legs were no help. I wasn't sure I even had the strength to sit upright. Dan must've wondered about that too because he reached across me and buckled the seat belt, holding me in the seat. "There's no body? What about that horrible smell?"

Dan shut the door and walked around the truck. He climbed into the driver's seat and started the engine before he answered. "I didn't say there was never a body. I said there wasn't a body anymore. Someone must have moved it."

I leaned my head against the window, saying another prayer of thanks for the cool of the glass. "Moved it into the bay you mean."

"Possibly."

"Then it isn't Frank. The body in the bay, I mean. It was Jack." A glimmer of relief helped settle my stomach, though I didn't like the thought of Jack being murdered either.

"Maybe. I checked on Jack after Frank went missing, but when I saw the sign and his truck was gone, I assumed he'd gone hunting like he does every year round about this time. Trouble is, everybody knows that, so it's possible they might have borrowed the use of the saw—" I groaned, and he looked at me. "What made you open the door?"

"I don't know. I came up here to talk to him, and I guess I just thought I'd leave him a note."

He nodded, then backed out of the lot. "What did you want to talk to him about? Same reason you called me?"

"Sort of. It's a long story. Are we just going to leave the mill like that? Don't you need to, I don't know, collect evidence?"

"I'll have to get the state crime lab down again. Tell me the long story."

"Can it wait until we get to Mel's? I don't think I can have this conversation twice."

We drove past the cabins. Taylor was sitting on a chair outside the cabin next to Frank's, watching the sunset over the bay. She stared at us as we drove by, but she didn't wave, nor did I. "What's that all about?" asked Dan. "You and Ms. Lennon have a falling out?"

"I don't know, Dan. To tell the truth, I don't know anything anymore. I don't know what to think or who to believe. A week ago my life was sailing along, peaceful and happy. Today? Everything's different. Everything's strange. Nothing feels like it used to feel."

"I wouldn't say that. Most things are the same as they always were, and you'll see that once this business is settled. Everything will go back to being the way it was."

"Will it?" I sat up, and the world swam, so I sat back and shook my head very slowly. "How can you know that?"

"Because this ain't my first rodeo."

I gave him a sideways look. "Nobody says that anymore, you know."

"I do."

"Well, you should stop."

Dan chuckled. "You see, Cara? Even now, as bad as I know you're feeling, you've still got your sense of humor. You wait and see. You'll come out the other end of this just fine."

"*A sadder but wiser Cara.* My mother uses that phrase, when someone we know has a bad experience that strips off some of their innocence. They'll be sadder but wiser for it. She always says that, and I never knew what she meant by it. I heard the words, you know, but I couldn't see the wisdom."

"Wiser would be good, but I wouldn't like to see you be sadder. I'll have to see what I can do about that."

I didn't ask him what he meant by that because we'd pulled up behind the restaurant and he was out of the truck and walking around to the passenger side almost before the sound of the engine died. He opened my door, and I stabbed ineffectively at the seat belt. He patiently helped me out of the truck because my sense of humor might have returned, but my sense of balance had not. He had to put his arm around me and half carry me to the kitchen door.

Mel had locked it again, but this time she answered on the first knock. She took in the sight of us standing there, Dan holding me up like a rag doll, and backed up to let us in. "Bent, come quick!"

Bent put down the spatula he was using to flip burgers, but Dan waved him off. "I've got her." He plopped me down in a chair Mel had dragged over from her desk in the corner and walked over to see what Bent was cooking. I was glad she'd grabbed a chair because I didn't think I could have managed a stool.

"Cara, my God, what's wrong? Are you hurt?"

"I'm fine, Mel, really. Don't fuss."

"She'll be okay. She's had quite a shock." Dan was leaning against the wall next to the grill, watching Bent sliding burgers onto the buns Mel had stacked with toppings. He scooped chips from the warmer and put a pile on each plate, then pushed them across the table to Mel. It was usually like ballet, watching them work, but this time their rhythm was off.

"Honey?" Bent tapped softly on the worktable to get Mel's attention.

"I… are you sure you're not hurt, Cara?"

"I'm fine. Go serve your tables."

She hesitated. Dan nodded reassuringly. She looked back at me, then picked up the plates and disappeared into the dining room. Bent put another burger on the grill and looked up at Dan, who nodded. Bent dropped two more patties onto the grill and then pulled out a package of thinly sliced turkey, setting it on the worktable. Mel came back and pulled down three plates, getting them ready. She asked only what we wanted to drink, before disappearing back into the dining room.

"Small crowd tonight, Bent?" asked Dan.

"Always is this time of year. I think we've only got three or four tables going out there." Bent added a serving of turkey to the grill.

"You're frying already cooked turkey?"

"For that one," he said, nodding his head toward me. "Normal people like bacon on their burgers, but Cara would rather have turkey."

"When in Rome," said Dan, looking at me. His gaze was oddly gentle. Bent grabbed another serving of turkey and added it to the grill.

"I like bacon," I said, finally finding my voice and being surprised that it sounded almost normal, at least to me. "Turkey is better. Turkey and bacon, now that would be good."

"Turkey's better for you than bacon," said Mel, coming back into the kitchen. She pulled a small pasta salad out of the refrigerator and went back into the dining room, returning with silverware and napkins. I sat watching her, feeling strangely disconnected from the normalcy of the kitchen.

When the burgers were ready, Bent piled my plate high with chips, and Mel brought in a pitcher of root beer. For once I wished we had something stronger, but I made myself get up and move to a stool next to Mel. Dan and Bent ate their meals standing up.

"So what happened, Cara?" asked Mel. I guess I must have been looking enough like myself that she thought it was safe to ask.

"Do you still have people out there?"

"Only a couple of tables. One's eating dinner, and the other's on dessert."

"Go throw pie at them and tell them to let themselves out when they're done. This is gonna take awhile."

She gave me a searching look but did as I asked. While she was gone, I thought about what I was going to say. So much had happened since I'd left that afternoon. I didn't know whether to put all the cards on the table, or protect Taylor and only talk about the grisly discovery I'd made at the mill. The mill was the logical place to start, but thinking about that would ruin my appetite, and Bent almost never made turkey cheeseburgers for me because he hated them. It might be selfish, but after the day I'd had, I needed my favorite food. I decided I would eat faster.

When Mel returned and had settled back onto her stool, Dan must have decided he'd given me enough time to collect myself. "Why is Ms. Lennon at the cabins?"

"Taylor's at the cabins?" asked Mel. "When did that happen?"

I finished the last bite of my burger before I answered, resigning myself to the ordeal of recounting my day. "We had a fight."

"Must've been a doozy. What were you fighting about?" Dan pulled a notebook from his pocket, reminding me that what I chose to say now might haunt Taylor forever.

"Were you fighting over Frank?" asked Mel.

"Why would they be fighting over Frank?" Dan and Bent asked in two-part harmony.

Mel rolled her eyes. "Because Taylor slept with Frank even though she knew Cara liked him."

"Cara liked Frank?" Again they spoke in unison.

"What are you, twins?" I asked. "Stop that. We weren't fighting because Taylor slept with Frank. We were fighting because now she says she didn't."

"No!" gasped Mel. "Why would she tell you she did if she didn't?"

"And if they weren't together," added Dan, "where was she that night?"

"I don't know why she said it, she just did. I don't know why Taylor says anything. She lied. When Frank turned up missing, she kept right on lying."

"Because she thought it was a good idea to lie to the police," said Dan, his voice dripping with sarcasm. "Why does everyone think it's all right to lie to the police?"

"This isn't about you, Dan," said Mel. "Go on, Cara. What is she saying happened now?"

"She said when she realized she was locked out, she started to come back here, but Jack confronted her. She says he called her everything but human until Frank stepped in. You remember me telling you he'd followed when Taylor left? Well, Taylor says he tossed her his keys and told her to go wait for him in the boat. She says he never showed up."

"I wonder which story is true."

"That's what I wanted to talk to Dan about. When my renter checked out of the cabin this morning, he said he saw Frank come home alone around two in the morning. If he took Jack home, spent a little time calming him down…"

"It still wouldn't have taken him until two in the morning," said Dan.

"Maybe it took a long time to calm him down."

"Or maybe Frank killed Jack," said Bent.

"Bent!" said Mel.

"Nobody's seen him since that night," agreed Dan, ignoring Mel.

"I thought you thought Frank was dead."

"Somebody's dead, Mel," answered Dan. "We don't know for sure that it's Frank. Could be Jack."

"Why would Jack be dead? I thought I heard he'd gone hunting." Mel looked perplexed.

"If Jack's dead," I said, thinking out loud, "where is Frank?"

Dan sat without answering for a moment, and I could see the wheels turning in his head. He knew better than to talk about a case under investigation, but he also knew that if he didn't tell them, I would. I guess he decided to spare me the gruesome task. "There's a lot of blood out at Jack's mill. Been there a few days, probably not more. Cara found it."

"Oh my God, Cara!" Mel threw her arm around my shoulders, nearly pulling me off my stool. "No wonder you were so upset."

"Cara, please tell me you didn't go up to the mill alone to confront Jack."

I tried, but I couldn't quite meet Bent's gaze. "I stopped by Dan's office first. Tammy said he'd gone home."

"And you couldn't wait? Or come get me? Cara, are you trying to get yourself killed?" I don't think I'd ever seen Bent angry. He was the most easygoing person I'd ever met, yet here he was, actually shouting at me.

"Bent, honey, keep your voice down."

"I know. I'm sorry. I thought about it, but I had my gun and—"

"And you've never shot a man with that gun. You don't know until you have to whether you actually will. It's not a choice I'd wish on you." I stared at Bent, openmouthed. I'd forgotten he was in the Navy. Maybe he'd done more than cook during his time overseas.

"Cara's learned her lesson, I think, Bent," said Dan, then he turned to me. "Good thing you called me, but if Jack had been there, and if he'd been our killer, I might not have been able to get to you in time to do any good. Bent's right. Hunting's one thing, but pulling a trigger to take the life of another human being, that's something else altogether. Any person with a conscience is gonna have trouble with that one, even when it's a question of your life or his. A second's hesitation could be the last mistake you ever have the chance to make."

I sat silently, letting the impact of their words soak into me. What a fool I'd been to go out there alone to talk to Jack, and now that I thought of it, it may have been equally foolish to confront Taylor the way I'd done. If she was the killer, now she knew I had seen her with someone who was obviously more than a friend. The heck with loyalty, it was time to lay all my cards on the table.

As expeditiously as I could, I told them everything. I started with the details the renter had told me, including his observation of the visits Dan had made to Frank's cabin, then told them about the scene between Taylor and the mystery man. I finished with the confrontation with Taylor that led to my decision to talk to Jack. The only thing I withheld were my own musings since they were only thoughts, and I was trying to stick to the facts.

When I finished, there was a long silence as the three of them digested what I'd said. Bent was the first to speak. "Dan, how fast can the state crime lab get here to take a look at the mill?"

"I'll put a call in to them tonight. If I know the boys at the lab, they'll head out at first light. Not every day they get to process a scene like that."

"Dan, that's morbid," I told him. Maybe I shouldn't have eaten so much.

"Maybe, but it's true. Every lawman lives for the opportunity to put their skills to the test. Not that we hope something like this will happen, especially to someone we know, but I'd be lying if I said it doesn't make your blood run a little faster."

"I understand," said Bent. "How long will it take to get a DNA reading so we know whether Frank or Jack is our victim?"

"This morning I would have said a few weeks, but now that Cara's found the scene of the crime, I'd say we just got bumped up the priority list."

"Okay, but you two are forgetting one thing." Both men looked at me. "I can see Frank killing Jack or Jack killing Frank in the heat of the moment if the two of them got into it when Frank took Jack home that night. What I can't see is why either one of them would… use the equipment at the mill… then dump the body in the bay. What kind of person does that?"

"Someone who's gone over the edge, Cara," said Bent.

"I agree," said Dan. "I get why the killer would want to cover it up, but this is more than a little extreme. You gotta be some kinda crazy to do a thing like that."

"So where does Taylor figure in all of this?" asked Mel.

"Yeah, that's what I was going to talk to you about. What kind of evidence do you have that Taylor was involved in Johnny's death? Or that his death was anything but an accident? And don't give me that crap about an open investigation, Dan. Taylor said you testified about this in probate court. Don't make me pull the transcripts."

"I spoke with the judge in chambers," said Dan. "All I said on the record was that I had reason to believe the death was suspicious and Ms. Lennon might be involved."

"C'mon, Dan. If I'm in danger, I think I have a right to know what you know."

Dan got up and walked to the door between the kitchen and the dining room. He looked first, then he went out without speaking, and the three of us stared silently at each other. He returned a few minutes later with another pitcher of root beer. After filling our glasses, he sat down. "Place is empty so I locked up for you. Now look, I know you three are friends of Taylor Lennon, but you were Johnny's friends too. If what I tell you gets back to her, you could be helping her get away with murder. Keep that in mind if she makes you feel guilty for not trusting her. She's real good at that, I hear."

He looked pointedly at me, and I blushed and looked away. Dan continued, "She told you Jack thought she had a lover. That's not quite true."

"She didn't?"

"No. She had a husband. Still has, so far as I can tell."

"What?" Mel's hand flew to her mouth in shock.

"Wait a minute, you mean Taylor was married before she married Johnny?" I asked.

"Before, during, and after."

"That would mean her marriage to Johnny was—"

"Illegal."

"Did Johnny know that?" I asked.

"I don't think so."

"Well, that's something, I suppose. It would have broken his heart," observed Mel.

"Better a broken heart than dead," I retorted. "Dan, when did you find out about this?"

"Not until after Johnny died. You know I would have told him if I'd known. It was Jack who found out about her. He came to me with the proof. He didn't want her inheriting Johnny's money because with that behind her, she'd be untouchable."

"What do you mean?"

"Money talks, Cara. It shouldn't, but it does. Hire the best lawyers, and if that fails, a private plane to fly you somewhere the law can't touch you."

"There's no way Johnny had that kind of money. Taylor might have, but she insists she didn't have nearly as much money as I'd always thought she did."

"That's where you're wrong. Ms. Lennon's fortune wasn't as much as you thought because it wasn't anything at all."

"What?"

"Ms. Lennon was broke when she married Johnny. Jack tried everything he could to get Johnny to do a pre-nup, but he wouldn't hear of it."

"Jack always said she was a gold digger," I said.

"I can't prove it, but I agree with him."

"How much gold are we talking about?" asked Bent.

"She stands to inherit close to fifteen million dollars in cash and other assets. That kind of money gives people ideas."

"Fifteen million dollars." The words sounded as impossible coming from me as they had hearing them from Dan. "Are you serious?"

"Dead serious, pardon the expression. That was enough to persuade the probate judge to give me time to investigate."

"And what have you come up with?" asked Bent.

"Nothing to hang my hat on. She was smart enough to live alone in Seattle, and she came back to Coho Bay alone."

"She told me she ran out of money."

"She probably did. Wouldn't have taken her long to run through Johnny's life insurance."

"But how could she have killed Johnny?" asked Mel. "You can't fake a bear attack."

"Oh, the bear killed him, that's for sure. I'll spare you the details of how we know, but take my word for it, the coroner had no doubt about that."

"So again, how could she have killed him?" Mel asked.

"That, I can't tell you. Just take my word for it that I do have a viable theory. I just can't prove it."

"So what about the man I saw her with?" I asked.

"If I had to guess, I'd say it's her husband."

"You said she came back alone."

"She arrived alone. He would have come separately."

"So who is he?"

"I don't know."

"What do you mean you don't know? You said Jack brought you proof."

"He brought me a marriage license. The name turned out to be false, and no one by that name is in Coho Bay now or then."

"Then how do you know she was married? Maybe Jack made it up. Wouldn't he be in line to inherit all those millions if Taylor were disqualified?"

"The license was real. I verified it myself. What was fake was the name of the groom and the ID he provided when they took out the license, but they tell me that would only invalidate the marriage if he was using a false name to cover up a reason why he couldn't legally marry her."

"Okay, so she was married. How do you know she didn't divorce fake ID guy before she married Johnny?"

"Whose side are you on?"

"The truth. Are you so sure Taylor's guilty that you're ignoring any evidence that says she's not?"

"I couldn't find any record of a divorce anywhere in the United States or Canada. She attested to the fact she'd never been married before on the application she filled out with Johnny, and when I asked her about it, she denied ever being married."

"What did she say about the license?" asked Bent.

"She said it must be fake, but if it is, it's a fake with her signature on it. And don't say it's forged, Cara, I had the handwriting experts at the state verify it."

"Is that all you've got on her?" asked Bent.

"Sadly, yes. This guy Cara saw may be our first real break. If I can track him down, I might be able to crack this case wide open."

"Well, if he exists, won't he be with her at the cabin tonight?" asked Mel.

"He exists," I told her.

"Possibly," said Dan. "I have the cabins under surveillance. Have ever since Frank went missing. If he turns up, we'll know."

"You have my cabins under surveillance?" I asked. "How?"

"Some things are better left unsaid. Anyway, I'd better be getting back out to Jack's. I don't have the mill under surveillance, so I'll have to keep an eye on it myself until I can get the crime lab in there. Thanks for dinner, Bent. Surprisingly good, that turkey cheeseburger. You oughta try it."

"No thanks," said Bent with a grimace.

Dan walked to the back door, then turned and looked at me. "Cara, I think you'd better plan on staying here, at least for now. Until I know who this guy is, I don't think anyone's safe being alone."

"You're going off alone into the woods to guard the mill. The killer could come back to make sure he hasn't left anything behind."

"Actually, I won't be alone. I don't want to say more than that, but trust me, I'm taking every precaution until we know exactly who we're dealing with. See you all tomorrow." He tapped his hat, a ball cap, not a knit one, and left.

"What do you think he meant by that, Bent?" I asked.

"I don't know for sure. I think he meant he has some men he can trust to have his back and that we're all safer not knowing anything more about it." Bent got up and started clearing the table, but Mel stopped him.

"You'd better go with Cara so she can pack a suitcase. If she's here for the duration, she may as well be comfortable."

I wanted to argue, but Dan had scared me again with all his cloak-and-dagger talk. I didn't want to believe that Taylor was the monster he was describing, but she had lied to me about Frank and she hadn't had an explanation for the man she'd been with. The truth can be told in a heartbeat, but a lie takes time to create. She'd probably have one by morning, but I didn't want to hear it. No, I was safer at Mel's, and I knew it, so I put on my coat and trailed after Bent without any argument at all.

"We have got to stop doing this," I said to him after we'd covered about half of the distance.

"We could always have your folks build a room for you in that house they'll be building behind the restaurant."

"You know we were just joking about that."

"You were, but they won't be. You wait and see. That's one thing Taylor wasn't lying about."

We stopped talking because we both realized there wouldn't be any building going on in Coho Bay now that the sawmill was out of operation. I shuddered and told myself it was because of the cold. I was glad once again that I hadn't gone inside. When we got to my apartment, Bent took my key and motioned for me to stand behind him. He tested the door first, and I was glad that it was locked. I don't think my heart could have stood another hair-raising search for intruders.

We went inside, glad to be out of the cold, and I hurried upstairs to pack. I would be working the next two days, the last two days of the season, so I put in two sets of the Coho Bay uniform. A few other necessities and some clothes to change into on the off chance that I would want to relax at the end of the day, and I was ready. Passing through the living room, I stopped. Hurrying to the bookshelf, I grabbed one of the few titles I hadn't yet read. Looking at the bloodthirsty cover in my hands, I decided to trade it for a romantic comedy. I rejoined Bent, who took my suitcase. When we left, we took care to lock the door behind us.

"You'll have to change the lock on that door," he said as we trudged back down the boardwalk.

"Taylor left her key on the counter."

"Doesn't mean she didn't have two."

I didn't answer. "I hate this," I said at last.

"I know. Don't worry, little sister. We'll get this sorted out, and life can get back to normal."

"Dan said something like that on the way back from Jack's place. I don't know that I'll ever go back to the way I was before. I feel like that ship has sailed."

"I'm sorry to hear that, but never say never. We'll see how you feel about things once this is over."

Chapter 10

Taylor woke me from a deep sleep, shaking me awake until I couldn't pretend I didn't know she was there. "Go away. Can't you see I'm sleeping?"

"Cara." Her whisper was something I felt more than heard. "Wake up, I need you."

"What? Why?"

"I need your help, Cara. I'm in real trouble."

"Why can't you be in trouble in the middle of the day like everybody else?" I complained, but I got up, shivering as the cold air in the bedroom hit me. I pulled on my jeans and a sweater and followed her out of the guest room. "How did you know I'd be here?"

"Where else would you be?"

Couldn't argue with that logic. "How did you get in?"

"Why do you have to ask so many questions? All you've been doing since I came back is ask questions. Why can't you just trust me?"

"You'd be easier to trust if you didn't keep lying to me."

"I never lied to you."

"You never stopped lying to me, Taylor."

She turned to look at me. "You never call me Taylor."

"It's the middle of the night. Where are we going?" More importantly, why was I following her when Dan had me half convinced she was a murderer? I took a step back.

"You know, don't you?" Her eyes flashed in the darkened stairwell. I saw a glint of light bounce off a blade in her hand. Where had that come from? "Dan told you about me, and you believed him."

"I don't know what you're talking about." I kept going backward, feeling for the next step and pulling myself up. Dear God, how many steps were there? I don't remember taking this many steps down. What would she do if I ran up the stairs? What if I started screaming? Could Bent get here in time? At least it would alert them to the danger so she couldn't get the drop on them.

"You little idiot." Taylor's voice was close, too close. I hadn't seen her take a step, yet her voice was right at my ear. "If you'd just kept quiet, I'd have given you a share of the money once the estate was settled."

"I don't want Johnny's money."

"It's my money! My money for putting up with that sniveling coward and his ape of a father."

"I thought you loved Johnny." That had been the one thing I'd been sure of when I hadn't been sure of anything else about Taylor. That had been the one truth that always made me forgive her, no matter how mad I got.

She started to laugh, but there were no fairy bells this time. She sounded like something out of a horror movie, right before the demented killer slashed another hapless teen. I pushed her as hard as I could and ran up the stairs. She screamed, and I heard her falling and screaming until she hit the wall at the bottom and the screaming stopped. Only it didn't stop. I could still hear the screams, but they sounded like they were coming from a long way away. Why was she still screaming?

"Cara! Cara, wake up! Honey, it's okay. You're safe."

I opened one eye, and when I saw Mel sitting on my bed and Bent standing in the door behind her, the other. It had been a dream. "Oh, Mel, thank God you woke me. It felt so real. Taylor was here. She said she was in trouble and she needed my help. Then she turned on me. She had a knife! I pushed her down the stairs. She was screaming and screaming."

Mel put her arms around me and rocked me as Mom had when we'd been kids and one of us had had a bad dream. "It was just a dream. Nobody's gonna hurt you, Cara. We won't let them."

I pulled away from her. "But that's the problem, Mel. I'm putting you in danger. Taylor said she knew I was here because where else would I be?"

"Cara, it was just a dream."

"I know, but it's true. If someone wanted to come after me, they'd know I'd be here. If they come after me, they could come after you."

"Nobody's coming after any of us," said Bent, walking into the room. "I'll put in some extra locks on the door tomorrow, and if I know Dan, some of those guys who've been watching Dan's back are watching ours."

"You think?"

"I wouldn't be asleep if I thought you or Mel were in any danger, would I?"

I looked at Mel. "Was he sleeping?"

"As far as I know. Didn't you hear the snoring?"

"That was you, not me," said Bent.

"Don't say mean things about the mother of your child."

I smiled, appreciating the effort they were making to calm my fears. Still, that dream had been so vivid. I didn't want to admit it, but I was afraid if I tried to go back to sleep, I'd be right back on those steps with Taylor and her knife.

Mel didn't need me to say the words. She pushed me over and crawled into the bed beside me. "Well, you're not going to be able to sleep tonight, and I'm too tired to stay awake. Honey, pull up a chair and keep Cara company, will you?"

"What, with your snoring? How's a guy supposed to hear anything over that?"

She stuck her tongue out at him but was asleep before he could retaliate. I looked over her to Bent. "She really does snore. Always has, even when we were kids. I used to think it was a bear breaking into the house."

"I'd go for freight train myself. Go to sleep, Cara. I'll take this watch."

"It's not fair to you."

"Walking in on that scene at the mill would give anybody nightmares. I'll sleep when the season's over."

"You'll have a new baby. You won't be sleeping then."

"I can do a lot of sleeping in five months." Bent reached over and switched off the lamp Mel must have turned on when she came in to see why I was screaming. I burrowed into the blankets and tried to focus on the familiar and safe sounds around me.

I must have been able to sleep because when I woke up again, I was alone, but the door was open and the light was on in the hallway. Bless Mel for knowing it would frighten me to wake up in the dark and find her missing after that horrible nightmare. She must have gotten up at her normal time and sent Bent to bed so he could at least get a little sleep before daylight.

I forced myself out of the bed and into the shower. I stood, letting the warm water rush over me until I felt it start to turn cold. I washed my hair in record time and stepped out just as the water was getting icy. Nothing like a cold shower to wake you up. I ran a comb through my mop of red hair and dressed for work. I spared a quick look out the window, was relieved to see the forecasted snow had not fallen, and hurried down the stairs.

Mel was singing to herself in the kitchen, and I stopped in the hall to listen. Bent was the more outgoing of the two, so Mel generally left the singing to him, but this morning she was belting out Aretha Franklin with abandon. She was making casseroles for the breakfast crowd, and I could smell pecan rolls in the oven. She whirled around, wooden spoon for a microphone, and stopped dead when she saw me. Instantly, her face turned red, her singing stopped, and her shoulders slumped.

"Oh, don't stop," I told her, coming into the room. "I like seeing you happy. I can't remember the last time I saw you sing."

Her face back to its normal hue, she switched off the radio. "That's because you sound like an elephant coming up the back porch every morning."

"Well, I must not be an elephant today."

"No, oddly enough. I heard you in the shower though. Bet you finished that one blue as a glacier."

"Just a little." I went over to check on the ovens. "You must have gotten up an hour ago."

"Had to. You were flopping around like a fish."

"I was not."

"I have the bruises to prove it."

I sat down on the chair I'd vacated yesterday. "Sorry. You start the coffee yet?"

"As soon as I heard the shower go on. Don't feel bad, Cara. You know I'm just teasing you. Truth is, I kept waking up to check on you, and, finally, Bent told me I may as well get started if I wasn't gonna get any sleep. I told Bent he could sleep in."

"I can stay and help you."

"You have to get to the gallery."

"I don't have a shipment to get ready this morning, and there's nothing left in storage, so whatever gaps I have on the floor are gonna stay gaps. All I have to do is unlock the door before the tender docks. I'll head out when we hear the whistle blow."

"Then I'll be happy to have your company."

Neither one of us said what I'm sure we were both thinking. I didn't want to be alone in the gallery until there were enough people around town to give me at least a sense of security. I went out to the dining room to set up the tables. I hated this fear. I was used to going where I wanted, when I wanted. I loved my little apartment, and I loved The Broken Antler. I didn't want fear to take that away from me, but I wasn't sure I was brave enough to face it this morning.

I was setting table three against the front window when there was a knock on the glass. I jumped, dropping a tray of silverware. Mel came running into the dining room, shotgun in hand. "What was that?"

"It's just Dan. He knocked on the window and it startled me. You look like Annie Oakley."

"Annie Oakley had a rifle, not a shotgun," said Mel, but she retreated back to the kitchen.

I stepped over the tangle of silverware and unlocked the door for Dan. "You scared the crap out of me."

"Good morning to you too."

"Good morning, Dan. You scared the crap out of me."

He laughed, which somehow made me laugh too. I stooped to pick up forks and spoons. Dan stepped around me and grabbed a fork or two and tossed them on the tray as we talked. "State lab boys are up at the mill."

"Already? It's not even light out yet."

"They dropped everything when I called last night. Look, I need you to keep this under your hat. I don't know who all may be involved in this, and I don't want word getting back to them that we've found the scene of the crime."

"I'm not anxious to tell anybody about it, but the gossip mill's gonna go crazy when they see the state police boat."

"They won't see the boat. It only docked at the cannery long enough to drop off the team and their equipment."

I sat back on my heels and stared at Dan. "Why the secrecy?"

Dan stood up and held out a hand to me. I picked up the tray and offered him my elbow to help me up. "Up to now I've had nothing solid about this man Ms. Lennon married. All I've had was a piece of paper, no picture, no description, nothing else to even say he existed, let alone had ever been in Coho Bay."

"And now Taylor knows that I saw him."

"She saw us together, coming back from the mill, so likely she put the pieces together anyway. They've gotta know the noose is closing in. That could make them desperate."

"More desperate than killing a man and cutting up his body? I still can't see Taylor doing something like that."

"I think you'd be surprised what people will do if they have the right motivation." He held up his hand to stop my protest. "I'm not saying she cut him up and tossed him overboard any more than she did the dirty work with Johnny."

"But this mythical husband of hers may have done both."

"He's not mythical. You saw him yourself."

"But we don't know he's her husband."

"We know that he was. What we can't prove is whether he still is."

"You said there was no record of a divorce."

"That I've found. Doesn't mean it isn't out there somewhere. Judge has ordered her to produce it, but as far as I know, she hasn't."

"If she did get a divorce, why can't she produce a copy of the decree?"

Dan took the tray and motioned for me to go ahead of him into the kitchen. "That's the fifteen-million-dollar question, though if she's convicted of complicity in Johnny's murder, it won't matter. She wouldn't be eligible to inherit."

"If it's Jack who's dead and for some reason Taylor is disqualified, what happens to the money then?"

Dan put the tray down next to the dishwasher and said hello to Mel. "For now, I need to know whose blood is at the mill, whether it matches our victim in the bay and whether that victim is Frank or Jack."

"I guess that's enough questions for one morning," I agreed. "While you're figuring that out, I'd better start making up new place settings so I can set the tables."

"When are you going to the gallery?"

"When the whistle blows."

"Call me when you're ready, and I'll take a smoke break."

"You don't smoke."

He grinned at me. "I could start." He nodded at Mel and headed back out the way he'd come.

"He likes you," she said after we heard the door chime.

"Tammy thinks I should go for him."

"Well then, I'll start picking out china patterns." That sent us both into peals of laughter.

Business was slow. There were lots of shoppers but not many buyers. End-of-season cruisers are bargain hunters, and none of the art I had on display was available for the prices that were being offered today. One or two collectors came in, and I negotiated deals on pieces I knew the artists didn't want to see back in their studios, but most of my day was spent making sure nothing walked away or got bumped off a pedestal or knocked off the wall.

There was an e-mail from the man who'd been interested in Johnny's work, but the price he opened with was far too low. I let him know that one had been taken off the market, so there was only one piece left. I knew he'd up his offer substantially, and even if he didn't, I owed it to Johnny to hold out for the best possible price. He was beyond caring about things like that, but I wanted his work to have the lasting respect it deserved, and high prices ensured the art world wouldn't forget about him. As I sent the e-mail, I wondered whether Taylor had really had something to do with Johnny's death.

If she'd been married before, I wondered why she hadn't told me about it at the time. She wouldn't have had any reason to cover it up. She'd said something about having a fight with her boyfriend, but Taylor was always having fights with boyfriends. She was forever falling in and out of love, but I'd never known her to be serious about anybody before Johnny. It had knocked me flat when she'd told me they were getting married. I'd had a hard time picturing her giving up her many men and settling down, but that's exactly what she'd done. Unless Dan was right and it had all been an act to get at Johnny's money.

Fifteen million dollars. The sheer enormity of that sum shocked me, but Johnny had never been much interested in the trappings of wealth. I wondered how

Johnny's mother had come by that kind of money and why the inheritance had bypassed Jack and gone to Johnny. I'd have to ask Dan about that. Father and son had grown closer after she'd died, not what I'd expect if your own spouse had disinherited you. That would give Jack a motive, maybe not to kill his own son, but certainly to discredit Taylor. Dan said he'd validated the marriage license, but what if he was in on it with Jack? What had Jack offered him to get Dan to stand up in court and tell a judge that what was clearly an accident might be murder? If they had the marriage license, that should be enough to disinherit her, as long as she couldn't produce a divorce decree. Why accuse her of murder?

None of it made sense. Yesterday had been the first real fight Taylor and I had ever had. If I were going to be honest, I'd have to admit it was more because I bit my tongue a lot around her than because we always saw eye to eye. I don't like conflict, so I turn away from anything that bothers me until whatever it is fades away. You can't be picking fights with people who annoy you in a town the size of Coho Bay, or pretty soon you'll be eating alone every night. It isn't that we never disagree, but most of us are of the "live and let live" persuasion.

Except somebody wasn't letting live anymore. I wondered how long it would take for the state lab to tell us which one of the two missing men was the victim and which was the killer. I'd been happy last night at the thought that Frank might not be dead, but now that I was thinking clearly, I realized if he was still alive, it meant he must have killed Jack. My head was aching, and it wasn't even lunchtime. The crowds started to thin early in the afternoon. It was cold, and many of them went back to their ship sooner than they might have had the weather been nicer. There was only one person in the gallery when Dan came in.

"Afternoon, Dan." Since I had a customer, I kept my voice light, as if our one and only policeman stopped by the gallery every afternoon just to say hello. The customer never looked up from the watercolor he'd been examining.

"Afternoon, Cara. Good day?"

"Always good when you stop by," I answered, unwilling to let the one customer I had think it had been a slow day. Slow days drive down prices. "Can I get you a cup of coffee?"

"I'd appreciate that, thank you."

I walked over to my customer. "Sir, I'm pouring if you'd like some."

"I don't want to put you to any trouble."

"It's no trouble. I see you're enjoying these watercolors. I know the artist would be happy to know she put a smile on your face."

"Is the artist from around here?"

"She lives just north of here."

"It's beautiful. Are you at all negotiable on the price?"

"I have a little wiggle room. Why don't you think about it while I'm getting your coffee, and let me know what you decide?"

"Thanks, I'll do that."

He went back to looking at the paintings. I smiled at Dan on my way to the back room, returning a few minutes later with three steaming mugs. One I left at the counter, one I gave to Dan, and the third I carried to the man who'd moved to the miniature of the town's massive sculpture.

I handed him his coffee and told him about the sculpture and the good work the proceeds were making possible. Except for some of the jewelry, the sculpture was the least expensive work in the gallery since it wasn't original. He ended up buying both the sculpture and the watercolor, for which he offered to pay full price. "I like what you're doing here, Miss King," he said as I rang up his purchase. "I've seen lots of galleries on this cruise, but none had the same feeling as I get in your Broken Antler. You care about the art and the artists, and it shows."

"Thank you, Mister…?"

"Bancroft. Steven Bancroft. Here's my card with the shipping information. It's been a pleasure."

"The pleasure is all mine, Mr. Bancroft. I hope you enjoy the rest of your cruise." One of the nicest things about running a gallery was running into people like him, who appreciated art and who didn't begrudge the artist a fair price.

Hearing the ship's whistle announcing the last tender would soon be leaving, I followed behind him and locked the door. I took down the "Open" painting and replaced it with the one that read "Closed." They had been a gallery-warming gift from Johnny when The Broken Antler had opened.

"One more day," I said to Dan. He'd stepped away during the transaction to give us privacy, and he was standing in front of Johnny's paintings. His face was thoughtful.

"I'm not busy," he said, "if you want company for dinner."

"Dan, I don't need a bodyguard."

"Who said anything about being a bodyguard? Maybe I don't feel like eating alone."

I laughed. "You been talking to Tammy?"

"What's Tammy got to do with it?"

"Nothing. She was trying to fix me up with you when I stopped by yesterday."

"Really? I'll have to thank her."

"You might not feel that way when I tell you why she thought I should go out with you."

"Why is that?"

"Because there's nobody else."

He put his head back and roared. Not the "that isn't funny, but I know you think it is so I'll laugh anyway" kind of laugh, but an honest-to-goodness belly buster. I didn't know Dan had it in him to laugh like that. I'd always seen him as a very serious, almost militaristic man with a permanent grimace from working with criminals all day.

His laugh subsided, and he rubbed the corner of one eye. "I needed that."

"I imagine it was a rough day for you. What did the lab guys say?"

"Not saying anything official until the report comes back, but they do think our victim lost his head at the mill. Who that victim is, we still don't know."

"Did you search the house?"

"Did that last night, but there was nothing surprising. Jack's hunting gear is gone, but everything else is there. The sign looked like the ones I've seen him make in the past."

"Which he would want us to think if he killed Frank."

"Or which Frank would want us to think if he killed Jack."

"True." I finished making out my deposit slip and slid it into the bank bag. My contracts with the cruise lines promised the gallery would be open every week of the season, but the first and last week were usually a bust. At least I hadn't missed having Taylor's help. "Shall we go?"

"In a minute. This guy you saw with Ms. Lennon. Are you sure it couldn't have been Frank?"

"We thought of that, but he was too short."

"How tall was he?"

"Taylor's about five-two and the top of her head was about chin level. I guess that would make him about my height or yours."

"Mine?"

"Had a coat like that tan one you wear with the wool trim. I'd have thought it was you except for the hat. And the fact that he was obviously on affectionate terms with Taylor."

"Glad to know you crossed me off your suspect list."

"You've also been in Coho Bay too long to be the man who married Taylor."

"So you did have to think about it in order to eliminate me as a suspect."

"Hey, like you told me, until I know better, everyone's a suspect."

"At least you were listening to something I told you."

I pushed him out the door and locked it. "I listen to everything, Dan, though you've been pretty quiet until now. Other than a food order, I don't think you've said ten words to me before."

Dan zipped his coat and waited for me to start walking, then fell in beside me. "I don't usually have much to say."

"You're from Homer, right? I think I remember Dad telling me that."

"Yep. Born and raised."

"And you moved to Coho Bay when your uncle retired. Why take a job in a one-horse town like this? Must seem dull."

"Have you ever been to Homer? Not exactly a hot spot. At least here I get the cruise ships coming in and out. New faces, new stories."

I stopped. "You like talking to the tourists?"

He stopped and turned to face me. "That surprises you?"

"It does. I'd have sworn you were annoyed by all the attention they give you."

"Well, you'd be wrong."

"This is a new side I'm seeing of you, Dan. Who knew you were a social butterfly? You're the only man in town who has a table to himself at Mel's."

"I'm not any kind of butterfly." He started walking again, leaving me to catch up with him this time. "Not true. Besides, the tourists treat me like I know a thing or two."

"I thought you told me once that tourists treated you like you were some kind of hick."

"A few do. I must have been having a bad day when I said that."

"I guess so. So why do you always sit alone at Mel's?"

"You probably don't know this, but Coho Bay isn't the easiest place to fit in."

"Everybody treats you like an outsider. Dan, that's terrible."

"It's not that bad, but when you're not from here, then you add being the only cop in town, and people keep their distance. Even honest people suddenly get nervous when I come into a room. People eat fast if I sit down with them, so I sit alone."

We reached the bank, and I tucked my deposit into the night box. "I'm sorry, Dan. You can sit with me tonight. Heck, if you don't I'll be eating alone, so you'll be doing me a favor."

"Don't let it get back to Tammy, or she'll have us picking out china."

Poor Dan didn't realize he'd stumbled across Mel's comment from this morning, so he probably didn't understand why I sat down right there on the edge of the boardwalk and laughed myself silly. There had been too much stress, too much tension, and the laughter helped break through some of that. Dan sat down next to me, watching me with a look on his face that set me off again. It must have been a full five minutes before I could breathe normally.

"You know, most men would be insulted if a woman laughed like that at the thought of marrying him."

"Dan, stop it, you're gonna make me pee my pants."

"Now that's romantic."

After another round of laughter, I was finally able to scramble to my feet and head across the street and into the dining room. The small crowd of locals barely looked up as I hurried through. Mel and Bent gave me a look as I sped by them into the bathroom, but they were used to me. By the time I came back into the dining room, Dan was sitting at a table in the corner, deep in conversation with one of the local fishermen. I guess he hadn't wanted to eat with me after all. With a twinge of disappointment, I climbed onto my barstool, and Mel slid a plate in front of me. "Not sure I should give this to you, but Bent said he'd already made it and it wouldn't be right to let it go to waste."

"Crab cakes? Whoo hoo! Tell Bent I'm all his if he ever wants to skip out on you." It was an old joke, and it made Mel laugh. "Why shouldn't you give it to me? What'd I do?"

"It's not what you did, it's what you will do. Crab cakes always keep you up at night."

"True, but what a lovely way to get heartburn. Worth every antacid in the bottle."

"Just you remember that when you're miserable tonight."

I dropped my voice to just over a whisper. "Trust me, I'd rather stay up all night with heartburn than have another one of those nightmares."

"Apparently Bent agrees because he's the one who set these aside for you. Those cruisers would have eaten us out of house and home if he hadn't."

"You're lucky. I barely sold anything today. Say, why do you suppose they're always so hungry? Don't they feed people on those ships?"

"I don't know, but I hope they stay hungry. We'll have another mouth to feed next season."

"One thing at a time, Mel. I have to get through one more day, then I can close up shop and focus on being the best aunt a baby ever had."

Mel smiled at me and put her hand over mine on the counter. "You don't have to do anything but be yourself, and that'll be plenty good enough for me."

"So what's Dan talking to Zeke about? Looks serious."

"I don't know, but it can't be too serious. He told me to serve him up here when his dinner's ready. Things getting interesting between you two?"

"Things aren't getting anything between the two of us. Dan's just keeping an eye on me because he thinks," I stopped, remembering the ears that were likely focused on us right now, "well, you know what he thinks. That's all it is."

"Sure." Mel went back into the kitchen, and I dove into my crab cakes. It's not fair that they don't love me as much as I love them, but considering how many I'd eat if I didn't know I'd be paying for it before morning, it was probably a good thing. The crab had been fresh caught in the bay that morning, and Bent had a way with spices that defied imagination. I would have loved anyone my sister loved, so long as he treated her well, but Bent's cooking made it easy. It helped that he was a nice guy, but the way to this sister-in-law's heart had definitely been through my stomach.

"Crab cakes? How do you rate?" said Dan, sliding onto the stool next to me. First Frank, then Taylor and now Dan. That was definitely not a lucky stool. Maybe I should warn him. We should probably play it safe and sit at a table. Except then the whole town would be marrying us off in the morning.

"Dad jokes that he and Mom helped open the restaurant because otherwise I would have starved to death."

"When's your dad getting back?"

"Should be here Thursday morning. Might make it home Wednesday night, but fortunately for the rest of us, they spend the night taking long showers before heading into town."

"Rough job, counting moose."

"Rougher than you'd think, but probably not as rough as your week's been."

"I've had better. I've also had worse."

"Really? I can't imagine what's worse than this."

"Let's keep it that way. I hear you're not sleeping so well as it is."

"Girl can't have any secrets in this town." I dropped my voice and leaned my head close to his. "What's up between you and Zeke?"

He leaned close to me and matched my whispered tone. "None of your business."

I sat up. "Not fair."

"Ongoing investigation."

"No wonder people eat fast around you."

"Now who's being unfair?"

"Guilty as charged." Mel dropped a plate in front of Dan before moving on to serve other tables. "Hey, you got crab cakes! How'd you rate?"

"I reserved them when I stopped by at lunchtime. I don't know what he puts in these, but I could eat them every day."

"I'm with you, but they wouldn't be special."

"I could live with that."

"So what's your story, Dan?"

"What do you mean?"

"Born and raised in Homer. You were a cop there, I take it?"

"Yep."

"Serve in the military?"

"Nope, went to the police academy right out of college, then joined the force back home."

"Where did you go to college?"

"Juneau. Criminal Justice."

"Then the police academy in Sitka?"

"It's the only one there is."

"Man, you're not much for conversation. I'm pulling teeth over here."

Dan put down his fork and took a drink of his coffee. I switch to pop after work, but Dan almost always drank coffee. Funny what you learn about someone when you work in a restaurant. I could tell you what foods he liked and how he liked it cooked. I could tell you what he didn't like and that he is allergic to peanuts, but I couldn't for the life of me tell you what kind of man he was. "I told you. I'm not much good at conversation."

"Okay. I'll just eat my dinner and stop bothering you."

"You're not bothering me. I just... I'm not very social."

"You're plenty social with the tourists. Just think of me as one of them."

"That's different. I don't have to see them day in and day out. If I make them mad, or if they get on my nerves, they're gone by sunset."

"So which are you afraid will happen with me?" He didn't answer. "You don't have to be anyone other than the person you are, Dan. I just thought that if we're going to be thrown together for the duration, we may as well get to know each other."

"I know you."

"I mean something other than the fact that we both like crab cakes."

"I know that you broke your leg when you were eleven, jumping out of a tree that anyone with a lick of sense would have known was too high to jump from. I know that you read enough books to stock a library, and you would have opened a book store except cruisers won't buy books, so you settled on your other love, fine art. I know that you love chocolate, and you have a stash of it in your sock drawer that you think nobody knows about."

"How did you know about the chocolate?"

"I saw it when Ms. Lennon was rifling through things looking for the clothes she'd been wearing."

"I was standing right there, Dan. She didn't look in my sock drawer. Her clothes sure wouldn't have been there."

"I didn't think so either. That's why I had my hand on my gun. If you missed her checking the sock drawer, you probably didn't notice that."

"I did, actually. I didn't know whether that was deliberate or habit, but I wondered about it. What was she looking for in my sock drawer?"

"I have no idea. She saw me watching her and slammed the drawer shut."

"There wasn't anything in there other than socks when I got dressed the next day." He raised his eyebrows at me. "Okay, socks and chocolate, but whatever it was, she must have taken it out after you left, when she told me she was going to take a shower."

"Did she take a shower?"

"I heard the water running, but I fell asleep on the couch before she came out. Why would she hide something in my sock drawer? She knows I wear socks."

"You have a good point there. Maybe she was putting something into the drawer. Something she didn't want me to find and didn't have much time to hide."

"If she had something to hide, she wouldn't have told you that you could have the clothes."

"Possibly. She might not have realized I was going to come with her and watch her while she got them."

"She did seem angry that night. I thought it was because you thought she killed Frank. I'd be mad if someone thought I killed somebody." I looked down at my plate. If it weren't crab cakes, I might have lost my appetite. "I think I liked it better when we weren't talking about the case."

"Hey, you're the one who told me I only know you liked crab cakes."

"Why do you know all this about me anyway?"

"It's my job to know about everyone, Cara."

"So who else in town is hiding chocolate in their sock drawer?"

He chuckled. "It's my job to observe. To listen. To put things together. Part of being a good cop is knowing who you can trust and who you'd better keep an eye on."

"And which category do I fall into?"

"Both at the moment."

"Gee, thanks."

"You asked."

"So since you're being so cryptic, let me ask you something else." I lowered my voice again. "Bent thinks you have people keeping an eye on us. He said it's so you know we're safe."

"That's not a question."

"You know what my question is."

He pushed his empty plate away and leaned back, being careful not to fall off the stool. Mel, who had a knack for keeping an eye on everyone's meal progress, appeared with two dishes of vanilla ice cream, trading them for our plates, then vanishing into the kitchen again. Dan dipped his spoon into his dish and swirled around the softer edges. "I think you should be on your guard. I don't think you're in any great danger, but I don't know that you're safe either. Truth is, there's too much I don't know right now for me to know anything for certain."

"That's not very reassuring," I said, picking up my own spoon.

"I could lie to you."

"No, don't do that. I've heard too many lies already. I'd rather have the truth even if I don't like the sound of it."

The room behind us fell silent, and I turned to look. I really have to stop doing that. Taylor was standing in the doorway, looking small and lost and frightened. Instinctively I started to move, but Dan's voice stopped me. "She's good, I'll give her that."

Good. As in acting. She looked genuinely distressed, but was it all an act? Had anything ever been true with Taylor? I slid off my stool and took my ice cream into the kitchen. "Taylor's here," I said in answer to Mel's unspoken question.

She looked at Bent, who put a burger into a to-go box and handed it to her. I leaned on the worktable, eating my ice cream, waiting for Mel to return. It didn't take her long. She pushed through the kitchen door, worry in every curve of her face. "She's gone, Cara. Dan too. I think he was going to run her back out to the cabins."

"Why was she here?"

"Why do you think? How else is she gonna eat?"

"She could buy food like everybody else. There's a microwave at the cabin."

"Which nobody ever uses. Besides, she held out a whole day. She must be starved by now."

"It's hard to have sympathy for someone who might have killed two men."

"You don't think she's a murderer, and neither do I. She's not your favorite person right now, and I don't blame you. I don't know what to believe with Taylor either, and you know her better than I do, but it's crazy thinking of her as some kind of siren, luring men to their deaths."

"It's crazy to think that two men have been murdered."

"Only one for certain. I still can't see how Johnny's death could be anything but an accident."

"What did Dan have to say?" asked Bent.

"Not much. The state lab thinks the mill is the murder scene, but they'll have to wait until the test results come in to know whether the victim was Frank or Jack."

"Or neither. It might be someone else entirely."

"Don't even think that, Bent," I told him. "My head hurts enough already."

"Just saying it's possible. We don't know anything for sure yet."

"That's what Dan said."

"Well, Dan's a smart man."

"He is a smart man," agreed Mel, "but is he a good man? If he's gonna be dating my sister, I need to know."

"Nobody said anything about him dating Cara. When did that happen?"

"Nobody's dating anybody," I said. "It's Mel's imagination."

"Well, you know what Tammy said. You're running out of options, Cara." There was a smile on her face a mile wide.

I threw a dish towel at her and retreated upstairs to the sound of her laughter. "Yell when you're ready to close, and maybe I'll come help."

"Where are you going?" Mel popped her head around the corner and looked up the stairs at me.

"I need a nap."

"Antacid's on your bedside table."

"Meanie!" I ducked into the guest room and kicked off my shoes. I lay down on the bed suddenly exhausted. Ten minutes later I found myself reaching for the bottle on the nightstand. Darn Bent, but those crab cakes were worth it.

Chapter 11

"That's it! Cruise ship season is officially over!" I announced to no one in particular. The final customer had left the gallery, and the last tender was loading at the dock. I grabbed my coat and locked the door, joining the other merchants and tour guides on the boardwalk. As soon as the tender arrived at the ship, a cheer went up along the dock. When the ship's horn sounded as it weighed anchor, music blasted from speakers hauled out from our one and only bar, and the town of Coho Bay celebrated the end of the season. We loved the business the cruise ships brought, and we enjoyed meeting the people who came ashore, but every year when the last ship sailed, we celebrated the sheer pleasure of having our town to ourselves again.

Every business closed its doors, and residents spilled into the streets for a buoyant block party. If you didn't eat at Mel's, I didn't see you from May until September, so I always looked forward to the end of the season celebration. It was exciting to catch up with friends, to hear the highlights of their summer and share with them what had been happening in my life. If you think not much could happen over a few months in a tiny town, you've clearly never been to one of our year-end parties.

Since it was too cold to be outside after sunset, the crowd edged toward the hall where the united women's groups of our three little churches were hosting dinner and dancing. All three congregations—Catholic, Russian Orthodox and Assembly of God—used the same building and rotated service times. They came together at least once a month during the winter, hosting events that brightened the endless twilight. This party had become a much-anticipated kickoff to their calendar.

By the thickness of the crowd in the hall, I'd say the whole town had turned out for the event. There are times when I am thankful to be a tall woman, and one of them is when I'm swimming in a sea of revelers. I was able to spot Bent easily. He was standing on the far side of the hall, part of a cluster of men who were hugging the wall as though it would cave in without them. Mel was more difficult to find, but I eventually spotted her at a table in animated conversation with her midwife. Childbirth was not an appealing topic of conversation, and I didn't feel like being the only woman at the wall, so I decided to join the line at the food table.

It was a long and slow-moving line, but I was soon hip-deep in shoptalk with a few fellow merchants, comparing notes about the season. I was glad to learn that the record-breaking sales at the gallery had driven sales for souvenirs, T-shirts and native crafts as well. I felt a tug at my sleeve and turned to find Taylor, who was looking up at me with pleading eyes.

"Cara, don't turn away." Her voice was urgent. "I need your help."

"Tay, I can't talk to you right now."

"Cara, please!"

I hesitated. I had reached the stacked plates at the end of the table, but my appetite fled as Taylor's appearance was twisting my stomach in knots. The room suddenly felt hot, and a wave of nausea turned me away from the food. The weight of the crowd pressing against me made it difficult to breathe, and I knew I had to get out of there. I mumbled something to the friends

I'd been talking with and pushed past Taylor, working my way toward the door. I didn't have to look to know she would follow me.

The blast of cold air at the door cleared my head. "How can you even ask me?"

"Please, Cara! I'm in terrible danger. I'll tell you everything, I promise."

I studied her face, searching for answers but finding none. She did look frightened, but a voice in my head was screaming that I couldn't trust her. "I can't tell when you're lying, Tay. Maybe everything about you is a lie. Maybe it's always been a lie with you."

"Cara, I swear. I'm telling you the truth. Every word."

I waivered. She sounded genuinely upset, but she'd sounded truthful before, and it had all been a lie. The nausea returned, and my head ached. I wanted to believe her. I wanted to help her like I'd always helped her, but there was a nagging feeling stealing over me that Taylor had only ever been my friend when she wanted something. Even if she was in trouble now, did I care?

Bent saved me from answering, stepping up behind me and draping a protective arm around me. "Something wrong here?"

My spine straightened. "I can't trust you, Tay. I don't know whether you're telling the truth, and right now believing you could get me killed."

Taylor took a step back, but she didn't walk away. "I guess I deserved that. I know I lied to you about Frank, and I've told you why."

"Which could also be a lie."

Tears glistened in her eyes. "I'm not lying, Cara. I'm in real trouble. I don't know what to do."

A chill ran though me as her words echoed the murderous ones of my dream. Maybe my subconscious knew her better than I did. "Dan's inside, Tay. If you're really in danger, tell him. I'm out."

I nodded to Bent, who gave my shoulders a squeeze and dropped his arm. I walked away, not knowing or even caring where I was going. I just wanted to get away from Taylor and was relieved when she didn't follow.

Mel must have noticed Bent leaving and came out behind him because she caught up to me before I'd gone even half the length of the block. "Cara, where are you going?"

"I don't know."

"Well, slow down. Pregnant lady here." She puffed out her cheeks and pushed her still-flat belly out, walking more like a penguin than a pregnant woman.

Her humor broke the tension, and I laughed so hard I had to stop walking. "You don't get to waddle for another four months."

"I'll waddle whenever I want to, missy," she said, trying to look hurt but not succeeding. As the laughter subsided, some of the anxiety returned, and Mel noticed the shift. She looked back toward the hall. "What did Taylor want?"

"I don't know. I've gotta get out of here. I'm not in the mood for a party anymore."

"We'll both go." Mel took my arm and walked back to where Bent stood. Taylor was gone, but Dan had come out of the hall and was standing with him.

"What did Ms. Lennon want?" asked Dan.

"Help."

"For what?"

"I don't know. She said she was in trouble. I didn't stick around to hear the rest of the story."

"Why not?" asked Dan. "Something going on between you and Ms. Lennon?"

"Nothing's going on, Dan. Nothing that involves me. She said she was in danger. I told her to go find you. That's everything I know."

Dan frowned. "I'll check it out. You two take Cara home."

"You shouldn't go alone," said Bent. "Let me drop the girls off, and I'll go with you."

I felt my heart sink straight into my shoes. "If you really think there might be something wrong, Dan, I'm the one who should go. She might not talk to either of you. Bent, take Mel home. I'll be there as soon as we're done."

"Cara, don't. Let Dan do his job."

"Mel, it'll be okay. Tay said she was in danger. She didn't say I was."

"You have your gun with you?" asked Bent.

"Locked and loaded." I patted my pocket, feeling reassured by the gun's weight.

"I don't like it," said Dan, "but I don't have time to argue. Where would she go?"

"The cabin?"

Dan nodded, and we set off at a fast pace, heading out of town and leaving Mel and Bent to walk home without me. I was expecting every moment to overtake Taylor, but we didn't see her. We walked the mile to the cabin in record time, but there was still no sign of her. While Dan banged on the door and shouted for her, a terrifying thought began to emerge from the fog in my brain. I staggered back from the cabin, stumbling my way out of the clearing and back to the road. I started to run and cursed the fact that I'd never taken up jogging as a hobby.

I was running as fast as my couch-potato legs would take me while Dan jogged effortlessly beside me. "Where are you going?"

My answer came in short bursts as my labored breathing would allow. "If Taylor really... wants help... she wouldn't just give up... and go back to the cabin... She'd go home and... wait for me."

"The apartment?"

I don't know if the pain in my chest was from fear or fitness, but I lurched, unable to run any further, struggling simply to stay on my feet. I bent over, hands on my knees, gasping for breath. "She'd know... I'm not at the... apartment. She said it... in my dream... She knew I'd... be at Mel's because... where else... would I go?"

"What are you talking about?" Dan shouted, exasperation in his voice.

I forced myself to take a few deep breaths before I answered him, feeling my heart retreat back into my chest at a more reassuring tempo. "It doesn't matter," I said as soon as I could speak. "Dan, we've got to get back there."

Wishing we'd taken Dan's truck instead of blindly walking to the cabins, I took another deep breath and forced myself to start running again. A mile never felt so far in all my life, and I almost cried in relief as I reached the restaurant. I didn't bother with the front door, which I knew would be locked. Instead, I rounded the building and hit the kitchen door at full gallop, twisting the knob and almost knocking myself out when the door didn't budge.

Dan caught me before I hit the ground and set me back onto my feet. I pounded on the door, screaming, "Mel! Mel, let me in!"

I heard a lock slide on the other side of the door, and Mel's voice sounded very distant. "Run, Cara! Run!"

I sprang back from the door and ran smack into Dan, who was an unyielding wall behind me. A few more locks slid and Taylor opened the door. "For heaven's sake, Cara, where have you been? I thought you'd never get here."

She was standing in the doorway, holding Mel's shotgun instead of a knife, but otherwise she was the image of the Taylor in my dream. She gestured for us to come into the kitchen, and I was shaking so hard Dan practically had to carry me. I heard the locks slide shut behind us, but as soon as we reached the kitchen, all I saw was Mel. She was sitting on a stool behind the worktable, her face streaked with tears. I managed to make it across the room on unsteady feet and threw my arms around her.

She sobbed against my shoulder. "She shot him, Cara. She shot Bent."

"No! No, please God no!" I turned to look at Taylor, Mel still sobbing in my arms. "What kind of monster are you?"

"I told you I needed help. If you'd just come with me when I asked, none of this would've happened."

I let go of Mel and took a step toward her. "Have you lost your mind? Dan! Do something!"

Dan didn't answer, but his eyes were focused on Taylor, who leveled the shotgun at him. "Take your gun out and put it on the table." When Dan didn't move, she racked a shell into the chamber. "Now." Dan's eyes narrowed, but he complied.

"Why are you doing this, Tay? Oh my God, did you kill Johnny too?"

"I didn't kill anybody!"

"You killed Bent," Mel sobbed.

"That was an accident!" Taylor snapped back at her. "How did I know Cara's gun didn't have the safety on?" She turned to me. "You should always put the safety on until you're ready to use a gun. Johnny taught me that."

It was surreal. There we were standing in the kitchen, having a normal conversation as though Taylor hadn't just shot my brother-in-law and wasn't pointing a shotgun at us now. My head hurt. My hand went to my pocket, but it was empty. "How? When?"

"At the hall. It was so crowded you didn't even notice me taking it out of your pocket. When you said you wouldn't help me, I thought I might need it."

"What? I had my gun with me after you left." I looked at Mel. "Bent asked me about it. I felt for it in my pocket."

"I don't know. I don't know," sobbed Mel. "He's gone, Cara. What am I gonna do?"

I put my arm around her again. "Why would you need my gun?"

"To protect myself."

"From who?"

"From Dan. He killed Frank and he's been trying to kill me!"

"What?"

"What are you talking about?" Dan and I spoke in unison.

"Either you did it or Jack did, and you've been covering up for him." She raised the shotgun again.

"Wait a minute," I said. "Why would either Dan or Jack want to kill Frank?"

"How should I know? Look, all I know is that Frank and Jack went off together that night, and now Frank's dead and Dan doesn't seem to be doing much to find the killer."

"That makes Dan a murderer?" I asked. "Sheesh, Tay, it's only been a few days. He doesn't even have a positive ID on the body yet."

"He knows. Everybody knows. If Frank's not dead, where is he?"

I turned to Dan. "She has a point."

Dan glared at me. "You're not helping." He turned to Taylor. "Answer her question, Ms. Lennon. Why would Jack want Frank dead?"

"Because he knew Frank was my husband."

Fortunately there was a stool in its customary place because I was so stunned I would have dropped right to the floor without it. "I thought you said the marriage license was a fake."

"It was real all right," said Dan.

"That means you were never legally married to Johnny."

"I divorced Frank before I ever met Johnny, Cara."

"You just said he was your husband."

"Ex-husband."

"Ask her where the divorce decree is," Dan suggested.

"You know I don't know where it is! When Jack showed up with the marriage license, the court ordered me to produce the divorce decree, only I didn't have it. I called Seattle, but the clerk said she couldn't find any record of it."

"Didn't you get a copy?" I asked.

"How can she have a copy of something that doesn't exist?" asked Dan.

"It does exist!" Taylor insisted, then turned her attention back to me. "I never got a copy because right after I filed, I moved up here."

"Oh come on, Tay. They would have forwarded it to you."

"I never thought to send them my new address. I didn't think it mattered."

"All very convenient," said Dan.

"Inconvenient, you mean," answered Taylor. "If I'd just had the decree, I could have shown the court, and the estate would have settled months ago."

"What a load of—you're not any more convincing with that shotgun than you were when you were telling that story to the judge. You expect us to believe that you got a divorce, but you didn't wait to see it go final before you married somebody else? Nobody does that."

"No, Dan," I sighed. "That's exactly the kind of thing she would do. What was he doing here, Tay?"

"Blackmail."

Dan slapped the table, and Taylor and I both jumped. Mel, in her agony, didn't seem to hear us. "Bull!"

"He showed up in Coho Bay, maybe a week or two before Johnny died. He told me he never signed the divorce papers and I was still legally married to him. He said unless I paid him off, he'd tell Johnny. I didn't know what to do."

"How did he know you were here?"

"You remember that magazine that did the story on promising young artists?"

"The one that put the picture of you and Johnny on the cover," I said.

"That's the one. Frank saw it. He said he dug into Johnny's background to find out what kind of guy I'd married. When he found out about the money, he must've seen his chance to cash in. That's all Frank ever wanted from me. He'd spent every dime I'd inherited from my parents, and now he was back to bleed me of whatever I could get from Johnny."

"Why didn't you tell me?" I asked.

"I was desperate, Cara. I loved Johnny. I didn't want to risk losing him."

"You mean, you didn't want to risk losing all that money," said Dan.

"Dan! Let her finish."

"Oh for crying out loud. You can't believe a word she says. Why are we even listening to her?"

"Are you afraid of what she has to say?" I asked.

"I'm not afraid of anything." Dan met my glare and raised me a grimace, but I held firm. He tossed up his arms in surrender. "Fine. Let her finish her story."

"That's all there is," said Taylor. "Before I could figure out what to do, Johnny died."

"Very convenient timing," said Dan.

"I agree," said Taylor, surprising me. "I was terrified, thinking Frank had killed Johnny. I spoke to the coroner about it, but he assured me Johnny's injuries were consistent with a bear attack."

I turned to Dan. "Is that what the coroner's report said?"

"For the most part."

"Why did you leave town, Tay?" I asked.

"And wouldn't Frank have followed you? Why'd he stay here?"

"I don't know. I didn't even know he was still here until I came back."

"That still leaves us with why you think Jack would want to kill Frank."

"When Jack contested the will, I begged an old family friend to represent me. I didn't have any money to pay him until the estate settled. I told him everything, Cara. You can ask him."

"Couldn't he track down the divorce decree?"

Dan broke in. "You can't track down what isn't there."

Taylor ignored him. "He wasn't able to find it in the database, and he didn't get any further than I had with the clerk in Seattle. He called me the morning before Frank disappeared to let me know he was going down there in person. He told me he'd search the records himself if that's what it took. I told Jack that when he confronted me in front of your apartment."

My heart started to beat a little bit faster. "Was Frank there when you said that to Jack?"

"No, he came up a little bit later."

"Dan, Frank would have heard that."

"If she's telling the truth."

"Granted that's a big if, but if she is, Frank would have heard that Taylor's attorney was going to Seattle to look for the divorce decree. Assuming the decree does exist, and the lawyer finds it, that would be game over for Frank. He had to get Jack to withdraw his objection to the will. You and I both know that wasn't gonna happen."

"It's a mighty skinny limb you've worked yourself out on, Cara."

"Maybe, but it would explain a lot of things."

Dan studied Taylor, who'd been looking back and forth between us as we talked, her brows knotted in bewilderment. "Let's cut to the chase. Frank's not dead. Jack is."

"What?" Taylor's face paled, and even Mel was shaken out of her grief enough to stare openmouthed at Dan.

"I'll tell you what I think happened," said Dan. "I think you and Frank are still married. If he left you when your money ran out, there's no record you ever filed for divorce. I think you came crying to Cara because you were broke and you knew she'd take you in. You wheedled your way into marrying Johnny when you found out he was rich, and you figured nobody'd ever know you were still married to Frank."

"I told you I didn't know about the money until after we were married."

"You've told me lots of things, and most of them are lies. I'll tell you something else. I don't think you ever stopped loving Frank. Whenever you found out about the money, you told him about it because you knew he'd come running to get a piece of it."

"She was married to Johnny for two years before Frank even showed up," I said. "He didn't exactly come running."

"Divorce decrees don't just vanish from court records, Cara. I pulled a copy of the license myself when Jack first told me about her being married." He looked at Taylor. "He was going to ruin everything for you, wasn't he? Frank killed him to save your worthless—"

"I don't know what you're talking about." Taylor looked like she was going to be ill.

"Jack hated you. He was going to make sure you never got a dime out of Johnny's estate. I don't think this pretty little scene between you and Jack ever happened. I think you sent Frank out there to kill him. Hell, maybe you went with him and helped get rid of the body. All we have is your word for where you were that night, and we all know what your word is worth."

"He's lying. Isn't he lying, Cara? Tell me he's lying to cover up for killing Frank."

I shook my head. "I found the blood at the mill."

"No, no. It can't be true," said Taylor, panic in every syllable. "If Frank is alive, he must've killed Jack."

"That's what I've been telling you," said Dan.

Taylor lowered the shotgun. Dan sprung forward to grab it from her, but she was beyond caring. She folded into a heap on the floor, rocking back and forth, holding her head in her hands. To my astonishment, Mel stopped crying and went to gather Taylor into her arms. "I thought he was dead," sobbed Taylor.

"I know, honey," said Mel. "I did too. We all did."

Dan said what I was thinking. "What the hell is going on?"

There was movement in the corner of the room, and I turned to see Bent walk out of the storage room. I screamed. Thankfully Dan caught me, or I would have joined Mel and Taylor on the floor.

"I'm sorry to scare you like that, Cara." Bent gave me a bear hug that did wonders for my emotions but nothing for my nerves. "Nice to know you'd miss me."

"I wondered where you were hiding," said Dan. "Is somebody going to tell me what's going on around here?"

"You knew Bent was alive?" asked Mel.

"Ms. Lennon said she shot him with Cara's gun. If she had that gun, why trade it for a shotgun?"

"My fault," said Mel. "I thought a shotgun would be more intimidating."

"I knew it! I did have my gun after Taylor left. You guys scared the pants off me!"

"I'm sorry, Cara, but we didn't have any way of letting you in on it without Dan knowing."

"So how come he saw through you and I'm the one who fell for it?"

"Because you take everything at face value," said Dan. "Why would you want to fool me?"

"Because I told them you killed Frank!" sobbed Taylor.

"And you believed her?"

"Well, as far as we knew, somebody killed him and Taylor tells a pretty convincing story," said Bent. "You knew about the mill, Cara. Why didn't you tell us?"

Before I could answer, Dan did. "I swore her to secrecy. At least I see she kept her promise."

"I always keep my promises!"

"And now I know that. What I don't know is what you all hoped to accomplish with this little farce."

"We thought if we could shake you up, you might make a mistake and let something slip that would prove you either killed Frank or you were covering up for Jack killing Frank."

"That was your brilliant plan?"

"I didn't say it was brilliant," admitted Bent. "Taylor was waiting for us when we got home, and she told us everything. We didn't have a lot of time."

Dan looked down at where Taylor sat, rocking back and forth, her eyes glassy. "Snap out of it! Tell me where he is."

"Do you think she's faking that reaction?"

"She's a world-class liar, Cara."

"I'm not lying!" Taylor blinked a few times, then scrambled to her feet and took my hands in hers. "You've got to believe me, Cara. I never saw Frank after he went off with Jack. I swear I thought he was dead."

"Why didn't you say something to me after you thought he was dead?"

"Because I still couldn't prove we'd ever been divorced. Honestly, Cara. I would have told you everything once my attorney found that decree. Before he left with Jack that night, Frank told me he was going to tell him who he was and that he was going to stand up in court and swear we'd been divorced long before Johnny and I got married. I swear I thought that Jack killed him to keep him from doing that."

"You said Frank was holding it over your head that you never got the divorce."

"He wanted the money, Cara. He needed me to inherit Johnny's estate if he was going to get his hands on it. I never dreamed he'd kill Jack. If I'd known, I swear I would have gone to the police."

"You're doing a lot of swearing, Ms. Lennon, but it's gonna take more than that if you want me to believe you," said Dan.

"Like what?"

"Like telling me where he is."

"How should I know? I said I haven't seen him since that night. I thought he was dead."

"And I'm telling you I can drive a truck through the holes in your story, so drop the lies and tell me where to find him."

"Everybody calm down and let's think logically," said Bent with a quiet air of command. "If Frank killed Jack, he went to a lot of trouble to make us believe that it was he who'd been murdered. What did he gain by doing that?"

"He didn't buy himself much time," I said. "Even if I hadn't stumbled into the mill, the police would have identified the body by DNA."

"Takes a few months to get those results," said Dan.

"Seriously?"

"It's not a TV show, Cara."

"I know, but months? It's Alaska. How many murders could they be investigating that our tests should take so long?"

"You'd be surprised, and it's not just murders. We have the highest suicide rate in the nation, and every one of them gets investigated as a suspicious death."

"Do you mind?" asked Bent, breaking in.

"Sorry," I said, feeling my cheeks burn. "You were saying?"

"He buys at least a few weeks by letting the world think he's dead and Jack's just gone off hunting. That's enough time for him to forge a letter to the court withdrawing the challenge to the will."

"But why would he need to do that?" asked Mel. "With Jack dead, wouldn't that serve the same purpose?"

"Not a chance," said Dan. "The marriage license was on file with the probate court, and the judge had ordered Taylor to produce proof that she had been legally divorced and eligible to marry Johnny. Jack's death wouldn't have changed that."

"But if Jack told the court he'd discovered the license was a forgery and he was withdrawing his challenge…" I left the thought hanging in the air.

"The judge might go for that," agreed Dan. "But that means Frank knew Taylor's attorney wouldn't find a divorce decree."

"Or that he would, and then he'd have no hold over Taylor. Stop the challenge, and you stop the attorney from looking for the decree."

"Cara, there was never a divorce. If Ms. Lennon knew for certain she'd been divorced, Frank wouldn't have had a hold on her. If there'd been a divorce, Frank wouldn't have even come to Coho Bay because he couldn't have known she wouldn't have seen a copy of it."

We both turned to look at Taylor. She tried to meet my eyes, but after a few moments she looked away. I tried not to let my mind go to the inevitable conclusion. There was too much at stake, too much left unanswered, and there was still a killer out there somewhere. Establishing whether Taylor was victim or partner paled in comparison with the urgency of finding Frank.

"Where would he go?" asked Mel, breaking the long, uncomfortable silence. "It's been too cold for him to have stayed outside. He'd have had to have sought shelter."

"He hasn't been back to the cabin, and he sure hasn't been here long enough to have made the kind of friends who would hide him," observed Bent. "His boat maybe."

"The boat's too public," said Dan. "Too easy for someone to see him."

"What about Jack's house?" I suggested. "Nobody would think to look for him there."

"Not bad, Cara," said Bent. "It's at the end of the road. Nobody would have driven by, and there aren't any neighbors within half a mile who would have noticed him."

Dan shook his head. "I went through the house after Cara found the scene at the mill, and I've been by there probably a dozen times since then. If he'd been there, he isn't anymore."

I felt deflated. "Where else could he go?"

"Any vacant rental houses?" asked Bent.

"There was one, but the owners came back from Texas last week. Everything else is occupied except the cabins. Tay, you were out there last night."

"Don't look at me. I thought he was dead. If I'd seen him, I'd have had a heart attack. I heard somebody come home in the middle of the night, but I assumed it was one of the renters."

"That has to be him," I said, turning to Dan. "The cabins are supposed to be vacant now. Let's go!" I relinquished my hold on Bent, who walked over to Mel and pulled her to her feet.

"We can't just go storming up there, Cara," said Dan. "Frank would be gone before we got to the front door. He must have Johnny's boat stashed somewhere, and if he makes it to open water, we might never catch up to him."

"We have to do something. We can't just sit here. Bent, think of something!"

"Like his plan to get me to confess?" snorted Dan. "No offense, Bent, but we need something better than that."

"Wait a minute," I said, turning to Dan. "What about those guys who are supposed to be keeping an eye on things? Let's get them in on this."

"They don't exist."

"They don't—What?"

"I made them up."

"You made them up?" I grabbed his jacket, bunching it in my fists. I wanted to shake or throttle him or maybe both at the same time. "You made them up?"

"I'm a one-man police force. It's better sometimes if people think I have a little help."

"I swear, I'm gonna kill the next person who lies to me." I emphasized each word with a pound of my fists on his chest.

Dan put his hands on mine and gently worked my fists open. "People are rarely what they seem, Cara."

"I have a suggestion," said Taylor.

"I'm not listening," I said. "How do I know you're not working with Frank? How do I know this whole charade hasn't been your way of trying to get us on your side?"

"Why would I do that? If I were working with Frank, wouldn't we have just marched into the courthouse and convinced the judge we were divorced?"

"Maybe you didn't think he'd take your word for it."

"Fine. Let's say Frank killed Jack and wrote that letter. Wouldn't I just lay low and wait for the estate to settle? Why would I have come to you for help?"

"You said you were afraid of Dan."

"I was afraid of Dan. Now I'm afraid of Frank. I'm sure not working with him."

"Bull," said Dan.

"Do you want to hear my suggestion or not?" Tay asked.

"Oh, by all means."

"We'll go to the cabin. You all hide, and I'll draw Frank out into the open."

"How are you gonna do that?" asked Bent.

"I'll think of something. If I can get him talking, maybe he'll admit I had nothing to do with him killing Jack."

"That only happens in books, Tay," I said. "Frank could kill you before we could stop him."

"He's not gonna kill his own wife," said Dan.

"Ex-wife," said Taylor, balling her hands into fists at her side. "He's not gonna kill me because without me he hasn't got a prayer of getting ahold of Johnny's money."

"You'd be taking a big chance," said Bent. "It's too easy for something to go wrong."

"Anyone have a better plan?" She looked around the room, but none of us had anything to offer.

Mel reached for her shotgun, but Bent stopped her. "You stay here. You too, Cara."

"I have to go," I told him. "I need to see for myself what's real and what isn't. Where's my gun? If Tay didn't take it—"

"I don't have it," she said.

"I do." Dan pulled my gun from his pocket. "That's the other reason I knew she was lying."

"How did you get my gun?"

"Took it when you fell into me."

"Why?"

"You won't like my reason."

"Don't lie to me, Dan."

"Every time I talked to you about Ms. Lennon, you defended her. Whatever she did or said, you found a way to excuse it. I wasn't sure whose side you were on, and I thought it was better safe than sorry."

"Dan Simmons! That's my sister you're talking about!"

"Sorry, Mel. She wanted the truth. Besides, you thought I was guilty. Why are you giving me a hard time for questioning your sister's motives?"

"He has a point there, Cara."

"Don't I get a gun?" asked Taylor.

"No," said Dan. "Not a chance."

"What is it going to take to prove to you that I'm telling the truth?"

"Tell you what. If he kills you, I'll believe you." By the tone in Dan's voice, I didn't think he was joking.

Chapter 12

For the second time that night, I found myself walking the mile to the cabins. Taylor had wanted to take Dan's truck but she was soundly overridden. The night was so still the sound of the engine would have carried and we would have had to abandon the truck halfway there to keep from being seen. Not that I blamed Taylor. I was thinking longingly of the truck myself as we slogged up the road. The snow that had been in the forecast for days had finally arrived, and it wasn't the pretty snow that made you want to sit by a fire with a mug of hot chocolate. It was a hard, driving snow, which gets into your face and makes it hard to keep your eyes open enough to see where you're going. We walked with our heads down and our bodies bent into the face of the wind.

I had a whole shelf full of mysteries at home, so to take my mind off the weather and the confrontation ahead of us, I decided to puzzle things out. I wanted to believe Taylor. She'd been my only friend that lonely year in Seattle. The fact that she was always more likely to act in her best interest than mine made her selfish, but it didn't make her a murderer. I could understand why she hadn't told me about her marriage to Frank. She'd never been one to admit her mistakes, and that one had been a doozy. I could even understand why she hadn't told me after he'd turned up in Coho Bay since by then she'd been married to Johnny and the sudden appearance of a blackmailing ex-husband wasn't something she would have wanted to broadcast.

What I couldn't excuse was her continuing to lie to me once she thought Frank was dead and Jack or Dan was trying to kill her.

She had been protecting the money. She might not have known about Johnny's wealth before they got married, but she was ready to risk her life to preserve her chance to inherit now that he was gone. Could I blame her for that? What would I do for a chance at fifteen million dollars? *What if she wants us to shoot Frank before he can tell us the truth about her?* It was an ugly thought, but my subconscious mind had been batting a thousand where Taylor was concerned, so I didn't dismiss it as quickly as I might once have done.

I looked over at her. I couldn't see her face clearly, but her stride was determined, resolute. What she didn't seem to be was frightened, as she had been back at Mel's. I was afraid, and I wasn't even the one planning to march up to a killer's hideout and knock on the door. Had she been telling the truth? Did she think he wouldn't kill her because she was his only chance at Johnny's money, or was Dan right and she was unafraid because she knew her own husband wouldn't kill her? Was she my friend in trouble or the murderous Taylor from my dreams, planning to lure Frank to his death? I shook my head to get the snow out of my face, but my thoughts continued to swirl.

We left the pavement as we drew closer to the cabins and went the rest of the way cutting through the woods. When we reached the clearing behind Frank's cabin, we crouched down to regroup. There was no light on, and we could hear nothing over the howl of the wind. Dan motioned for me to circle to the far side of the cabin while he moved off in the opposite direction. Bent stayed where he was, guarding the back. Once she saw we were in place, Taylor stood up and walked straight across the clearing and around the cabin to the front door.

I could only see the outline of her body through the storm, and I could barely hear her. I moved closer, pressing myself against the side of the cabin. If Taylor needed me, I wanted to be in position to act quickly. I heard her knock on the door, but there was no answer. She knocked again, louder this time, and I could clearly hear her voice. "Frank? It's me, Taylor. Open up." Still nothing. "Frank, I know you're here. Open the door. I'm in real trouble."

I flinched at her words, so like the ones she'd spoken to me at the party. She sounded painfully honest, with a hint of fear and vulnerability, only this time I knew it was a lie. Even if it turned out she were innocent, something told me I would never be able to trust her again. The door opened, and I realized I hadn't really expected Frank to be there until I heard him tell her to get inside before someone saw her.

I inched my way along the wall to the window, careful to make no noise as I moved. I knew the storm would cover most sounds, but I didn't want to take chances where Taylor's safety was concerned. I listened at the window but couldn't hear anything from inside. Steeling myself to look, I hoped that for once Frank had forgotten to close the blinds. They were open but only slightly. I could only see slivers through the slats in the blinds. It was dark inside, but I could make out two shapes. The smaller seemed to be struggling to break away from the larger. Then I heard Taylor scream, and that was enough for me. I shattered the window with the butt of my gun and made a sound that would have made a warrior proud. I heard another window break and the sound of Dan battering at the door. Frank spun Taylor around and pinned her in front of him. "Back off! All of you! Back off or I'll blow her head off!"

"Let her go!" I screamed.

"Porch, Cara. Now!" said Frank, recognizing my voice. "You too, Dan. I want you where I can see you."

I moved to the porch, my gun drawn and ready. Dan stood by the door, tensed to pounce when Frank and Taylor came out. I didn't see Bent, and since Frank had only mentioned me and Dan, maybe he didn't realize we had a third person. That could be the difference between life and death for Taylor. I gripped my gun tightly and tried to ignore the snow swirling all around me. At least here under the porch overhang I wasn't getting blasted with snow pellets as I had all the way up to the cabins.

"Open the door, Cara," ordered Frank, "and don't try anything."

I opened the door and backed away from it, but I didn't lower my gun and neither did Dan, who stood behind me and to my left. Frank was standing about six feet into the one-room cabin, holding Taylor in front of him, a gun to her temple. It was too dark to see their faces, but I could see her squirming in his grip until Frank jerked the arm he held around her waist and she stopped moving. "Put down your guns," he ordered. "Don't even think about it, Dan."

I stole a glance at Dan. His face was a mask, but he bent down slowly and placed his gun on the porch. He nodded at me, and reluctantly I put my gun beside his and we backed carefully off the porch. I said a silent prayer of thanks that we still had Bent hidden out there, somewhere, watching and waiting for the right time to move in. Dan and I stood at the foot of the steps and watched while Frank dragged Taylor out of the cabin. She was sobbing with a terror I didn't think she could fake. Whatever she might have done, it seemed clear she was not Frank's partner in crime. I breathed a little easier at that, or I would have if the wind weren't catching every breath almost before I could exhale.

"You'll never get away with it, Frank." I marveled at the calm in Dan's voice. I guess that's why he's a cop and I'm a gallery owner. "Let her go before you make things worse for yourself."

"You want her? Take her." To my amazement, Frank relinquished his hold on Taylor and she collapsed onto the deck at his feet. Before I could take a step to reach her, she'd half crawled, half fallen down the steps and thrown herself at Dan. Her arms went around his neck, and she hung there, sobbing on his shoulder.

"She's no good to you now, Dan," said Frank, lowering his gun.

"What are you talking about?" I asked, having to shout to be heard above the storm. Frank stood there in his shirtsleeves, impervious to the cold, his full attention on Dan.

"She'll never inherit that estate now. You know that." Dan still hadn't moved. One arm was around Taylor and the other hung at his side. He said nothing.

I caught movement out of my eye and turned to look beyond Dan and Taylor. I almost cried with relief when I saw Bent moving toward us, shotgun ready. He was too far away to have a clear shot. *Keep him talking, Dan. Just a little bit longer.* I hoped Frank hadn't seen my head turn.

Dan's hand flew to his belt, and he pulled something out of a small holster. Metal glinted, and I realized he held a collapsible hunting knife. I was relieved to see it, but I didn't know how he was going to take on Frank, who still had a gun, with a knife. I looked around wildly, but Bent seemed to have faded into the storm.

"Go ahead and kill her," shouted Frank.

"Frank! What the—"

"Cara, don't you get it?" Frank shouted back at me. "He's killed two men to get that money."

Taylor pulled away from Dan and stood staring at him. "Two men?"

"Jack and Johnny. You killed them both, didn't you Dan?"

"Johnny?" Taylor turned to look at Frank, but she didn't move away from Dan. "Johnny was killed by a bear."

"Frank, what are you talking about?" I demanded. "The coroner called it a bear attack. You can't fake those kind of injuries."

"There were other injuries that didn't fit. The coroner dismissed them, but Jack didn't, did he, Dan? Jack suspected you right from the start. That's why he called me."

"He... what?" Now it was Taylor's turn to be confused.

Dan grabbed Taylor and gestured at Frank with his knife. "Then shoot us both! Go on, do it. Bent! Where are you?" He spun around, waving the knife wildly. Taylor screamed and fought him, but she couldn't break his grip.

"No! Stop it, both of you!" I cried.

Frank ignored me. "Give it up, Dan. Even if you get out of Coho Bay, where are you going to go? You have Johnny's boat, but you don't have any money. The police will freeze your credit cards before you can make it to Canada."

"I'll take my chances. Put your gun down or shoot us. Either way, I'm ending this!" Taylor screamed as Dan pressed the knife to her neck, drawing blood.

I couldn't stand it. Friend or foe, nobody deserved to die like this. "Please, Frank, let them go! Don't just stand there and let him kill her."

"Cara, she's a killer, every bit as much as he is." Frank's voice was harsh. "She suspected he killed Johnny, and she did nothing. She knew he killed Jack, and still she did nothing. Don't you believe me?"

"I don't know what to believe anymore!"

Frank waivered, then threw his gun away with a grunt of disgust. "Fine. Take her. Get out of here."

"Not quite." Dan shouted into the storm. "Bent! Where are you?"

"Right here, Dan."

I almost sobbed in relief when Bent emerged from the storm. He stood between me and Frank, shotgun in hand, but he didn't raise it. Dan tightened his hold on Taylor, almost lifting her off the ground. "Tell them!"

"Let me go!" she sobbed.

"Tell them or I slit your throat! Tell them what you did to Johnny!"

"I didn't..." She gasped for air.

"You lying sack of—" He threw her to the ground. "Shoot her, Bent!"

"No!" Taylor and I screamed, but I stayed rooted to the ground, watching in horror as Bent pointed his shotgun at her and racked a shot into the chamber.

Taylor raised her hand in a feeble attempt to block the shot. "It was an accident! I swear it! I didn't mean to kill him."

If I were the fainting type, I would have fainted then. As it was, my legs lost the strength to hold me, and I sunk into the snow. I felt, more than saw, Frank move over to stand behind me. "She was at the gallery..." I stopped. I didn't know what to say.

"She wasn't there all day, were you?" Dan prodded Taylor with his foot. "You slipped away from the gallery and went up to where you knew Johnny would be."

"I had to. I had to make him see. He wouldn't listen to me."

"I don't understand," I said, my voice sounding strange even to me.

Taylor looked at me, her face pleading. "Jack knew about Frank. I don't know how he found out, but he went to Johnny with the marriage license. I told Johnny we were divorced, but he didn't believe me."

"I wonder why," said Frank.

"I thought we were! I swear I did. I filed. I don't know what happened. When Frank showed up, I got scared."

"So Frank really is your husband."

"Ex-husband! I told Johnny that, but he was so mad. He just walked away from me. I went after him. I grabbed his arm to stop him but he... he pulled away... He fell." She stopped, and there was nothing but the sound of the storm while she gathered her thoughts. "I know I shouldn't have left him there, but I was scared. I thought I'd killed him. I just ran away."

"And left him there, bleeding and unconscious in a known bear area," Frank finished her story.

"I didn't think! I was so scared I just didn't think."

"Except it wasn't an accident, was it?" Dan kicked her again. "He didn't just fall, did he? You shoved him over that ledge. We found his body at the bottom of a thirty-foot drop."

Taylor lay on the cold, wet ground sobbing. "I didn't mean it. I didn't mean it. I just... lashed out. I swear I didn't mean to kill him."

"That enough for you?" I looked to see who Dan was talking to. He was looking behind me but to the right. I turned to see Jack, emerging from the storm.

"That'll do," he said. I don't remember anything else.

Chapter 13

I was crating up unsold paintings and sculptures for shipment back to the artists who'd created them. I was late getting the work done, but it had been a crazy two weeks. I heard a knock on the gallery door, and Frank held up a bag and gestured for me to unlock the door. I walked to the entry slowly. I'd been doing everything slowly since that night at the cabins. I wondered if I'd ever feel normal again.

"I thought you were taking off today," I said, standing back to let him come in.

"I am. I stopped in at the restaurant to say good-bye, and Mel bribed me with lunch if I could get you to eat something."

"Mel worries too much."

"She worries about you."

"She doesn't need to. I'm fine."

"I won't tell you what we said 'fine' stood for in the Marines." He walked ahead of me into the back room and unpacked the bag. Two burgers, beef, since Bent had run out of wild game. I could hardly wait to join Dad and Bent on our first moose hunt of the season. We'd head out as soon as I got the gallery buttoned up for the winter.

I took the burger Frank held out to me and sat down at my desk. I hadn't realized I was hungry until I smelled the food. "I didn't know you were in the Marines."

"There's a lot you don't know about me."

"I guess there's a lot I never will know with you heading back to Seattle."

"Maybe."

I stopped eating. "Maybe?"

"I have a few things to take care of, but I've been thinking about moving back here."

My throat suddenly felt dry. "You have?"

"Jack's been talking to me about taking over the mill. With Johnny gone, he doesn't have the heart for the work anymore."

"I still can't get over it. From the very first day, he knew Taylor killed Johnny only nobody believed him."

"Dan did. I did. We just couldn't prove it. She had you as an alibi. We didn't know if you were lying to protect her or if she'd slipped out without you knowing she was gone."

"I've wracked my brain. I still don't remember her being gone that day, but I checked my receipts. It was crazy busy. Why did she come back? Why didn't she just stay in Seattle after Johnny died?"

"Because she had to take care of Jack. He was challenging the will, and he kept writing to her, telling her he knew she was lying about being divorced. He told her he'd find her first husband and haul him into court to show the judge she was never legally able to marry Johnny."

"But you are her first husband. You were already here."

"She didn't know that Jack knew who I was. When he found me in Seattle, I told him the truth. I divorced Taylor when I realized what a snake I'd married. He said she hadn't produced the decree, so I got a friend of mine who works for the court to delete it from the system and misfile the hard copy. I came to Coho Bay at Jack's request. He hoped I could rattle her into leaving Johnny, and if that didn't work, maybe I could convince Johnny that Taylor and I were still married."

"Which would have been a lie."

"And a kindness to Johnny, getting Taylor out of his life."

"A kindness that ended up costing him his life."

"We never dreamed she'd kill him." Frank's eyes clouded, and neither of us spoke for a long time. "From that moment on, we knew we had to get her to confess. It was the only way."

"So Jack bullied her when she came back. He didn't think that would break her, did he?"

"Jack did a lot of drinking after Johnny died. He didn't always think too clearly. I told Dan everything after that night at Mel's. I needed his help to put pressure on Taylor."

"So Dan went after her romantically? Then it was him I saw her with behind the gallery."

"Taylor's a champion at wrapping men around her finger and getting them to do things for her. If we could get her to believe Dan was under her spell, she might let her guard down."

"Why fake Jack's death?"

"We had to turn up the pressure. If her lawyer found that divorce decree, the estate would settle, and she'd take the money and run. We had to convince her that Jack was so out of his mind with grief that he'd killed me and would be coming after her."

"How did you get the state police to go along with the body in the bay story?"

He chuckled. "Dan cashed in every favor he had pulling that one off. Even managed to swear the crab fisherman to secrecy in exchange for tearing up a citation, that's the one that impressed me. He's a pretty persuasive guy."

"And the scene at the mill?"

"We staged it. We assumed Taylor would go out to the mill to confront Jack when I went missing."

"Only she didn't. I did." I pushed away. "You can't fake those flies. And that smell," I shuddered.

"I'm sorry, Cara. We had to make it convincing. Fortunately, there isn't much difference between rancid human blood and rancid . . ."

I put up my hand. "I don't want to know. What about the lab crew? How many favors did that cost Dan?"

"None. He never called them."

"Lies. Always back to lies. Taylor thought Dan was in on it with Jack. Why would she believe he'd suddenly fallen for her?"

"Never underestimate that woman's vanity. Dan had her convinced . . ."

"I still don't get it. Taylor thought Dan was in on it with Jack."

"No, Dan had her convinced Jack was on a rampage and that since you kicked her out, you and your family were starting to doubt her. She needed you on her side because you were her alibi for Johnny's death. She couldn't take a chance that you'd start going over that day in your head and remember a time when you'd looked for her but she hadn't been there. Dan and I cooked up the scene at Mel's, and she took the bait, thinking it was the only way to convince you she was innocent."

"And her reaction to finding out that it was Jack who was dead, not you?"

"Shows you what we were up against. That had to have freaked her out, but she got over it fast and jumped at the chance to pin everything on me. If she could trick you or Bent into shooting me, I wouldn't be able to tell people we were never divorced."

"At least I was right about something. I wondered at the time if she was setting you up."

"Really? I would have sworn you believed her. We had a heck of a time getting Mel and Bent to go along with us, but we couldn't let them tell you what the plan was. You're not a very good liar, and we needed your reactions to be genuine in order to convince Taylor."

"I guess there's been a part of me that has been questioning Taylor's motives ever since she came back. Something about it just felt wrong, and I kept getting the feeling she was lying to me. I tried to shake it off, but it wouldn't shake."

"You're a trusting soul, Cara. Nothing wrong with that."

"Speaking of trusting, what was all that crap with Mr. Shoes?"

Frank looked puzzled for a moment, then he smiled. "Sorry. When you welcomed Taylor back with open arms, I wasn't sure whose side you were on. I wanted to shake you up a bit."

"But I saw someone down there."

"That was Dan. I left him in front of city hall when I went up to check on you. When I noticed all you could see was his legs, I decided it wouldn't hurt to keep you a little off-kilter, in case you were helping Taylor. Even if you weren't, I knew you'd tell her about it and it would make her think somebody was keeping an eye on her."

"And later? When I thought someone was at my door?"

He held up his hands. "Guilty as charged. By then I was pretty sure you weren't in on it and I didn't think it was safe for you to be sharing an apartment with her. I had to scare you in order to get you to go stay with Mel and Bent. I didn't know until later that she wasn't even there that night."

I picked up the trash left behind from lunch and tossed it into the garbage. "Will she go to prison?"

"I hope so. Depends on whether she has a good lawyer."

"She's a good liar. She'll find a way to talk herself out of this."

"She might. She won't ever get Johnny's money, though and without it, she's stuck with a public defender. Hopefully a crappy one. Time will tell."

"I talked to Jack yesterday. He wants me to have Johnny's boat and the house on the island."

"He told me he was going to offer them to you."

"I took the boat. Dad's is in terrible shape, and we need a reliable one in case Mel has to go to the hospital to have the baby."

"And the house?"

"I asked him to let me use it as an artist's retreat. I thought every summer I could invite a promising artist to work on the island. Johnny would have liked that."

"I'm sure he would have."

I walked back into the gallery and stood in front of Johnny's paintings. They would stay on the wall for now until Jack decided what he wanted to do with them. Looking up at them, my heart ached for my childhood friend. I, too, shouldered a share of the blame for his death since Taylor would have never come to Coho Bay except to see me. "So are you really going to take over the mill?"

"Think I should?" Frank had come up to stand behind me. He put his hands on my shoulders, and I leaned back against him, appreciating his nearness.

"Yes. Yes, I do."

THE END

ABOUT THE AUTHOR

Linda Crowder is best known for her *Jake and Emma Mystery* series, set in her adopted home town of Casper, Wyoming. The series features a pair of accidental detectives who join forces with the local police to track down killers. Her books are a delightful blend of mystery, relationships, humor and tears. Linda and her husband fell in love with Alaska on their first trip there in 2014. Her love of the Alaskan Inside Passage led her to place the *Caribou King Mystery* series in the mythical cruise ship town of Coho Bay, Alaska

From the Author

Thank you for reading my book about the people in Coho Bay, Alaska. The Inside Passage is one of the most beautiful places on earth and it's my pleasure to bring it into your home. I was there last in May 2016 and saw whales, seals, sea lions and more eagles than I could count. The people are some of the most friendly I've met and I appreciate all of them who took the time to answer my questions about what it's like to live in this northern paradise.

If you enjoyed *The Fine Art of Deception*, I would appreciate if you posted a quick review on your favorite book website. If you visit my website, http://www.lindajcrowder.com/ sign up for my newsletter so I can let you know when *The Fine Art of Love and Murder*, is ready.

Can't wait? You might enjoy my other series, *Jake and Emma Mysteries*. Jake and Emma Rand are a couple of accidental detectives who are forced into catching killers when they find the body of a woman on their fence line in Casper, Wyoming. To meet Jake and Emma, look for *Too Cute to Kill* at your favorite book seller.

Other books by Linda Crowder

Jake and Emma Mysteries:

Too Cute to Kill
Main Street Murder
Justice for Katie
Death Changes Everything
Coming soon: *A Body on the Ballot*

Short Stories

Ringo the Ghost Cat
Boots
Lindsey

www.ingramcontent.com/pod-product-compliance
Lightning Source LLC
Chambersburg PA
CBHW020313260626
47156CB00004B/1206